HALF

as

HAPPY

HALF

as

HAPPY

GREGORY SPATZ

Engine Books
Indianapolis

Engine Books
PO Box 44167
Indianapolis, IN 46244
enginebooks.org

Thanks to the following journals where some of these stories originally appeared in somewhat different form: "Any Landlord's Dream," "Happy For You," and "A Bear For Trying," *New England Review;* "No Kind of Music," *Glimmer Train Stories;* "Luck" and "String," *Epoch;* "The Bowmaker's Cats," *Kenyon Review;* "Half as Happy," *Northwest Review.*

Also available in eBook formats from Engine Books.

Printed in the United States of America

10   9   8   7   6   5   4   3   2   1

ISBN: 978-1-938126-09-3

For Caridwen

CONTENTS

Any Landlord's Dream	9
Happy For You	37
No Kind of Music	55
Luck	87
The Bowmaker's Cats	103
A Bear For Trying	117
Half as Happy	139
String	163

ANY LANDLORD'S DREAM

THEY WERE NOT THE FIRST. In fact, the house had stood empty for several months and the landlord was ready to bargain. The walls had given up the smells of the most recent tenants; other scents, long buried under paint and wallpaper and more paint and more wallpaper, had come again to prevail, though reduced by time to more generalized versions of whatever accident or incident caused them, so, coming in the front door, one no longer sniffed and said, *patchouli, burnt steak, flea bomb,* or even *death,* but instead, after a breath or two, felt a vague hunger or dislike or worry and commented in such terms as *sour, musty, needs fresh paint,* or *do these windows open?* Words were some help: brick, 1920, one-story, finished basement, remodeled kitchen, gas oven, built-ins, original gum wood doors and trim, arched doorways, recessed lighting, breakfast nook, semi-attached workshop and garage. It was not the same, though, as standing there and seeing yourself anew in new surroundings. The ones who had come the closest so far were a younger, unmarried couple who first peeked through the windows late on a Sunday afternoon and returned again a few days later during regular working hours to let themselves in with a key on a green shoe string given to them by the landlord in his downtown office. These two were so charged, picturing the life they'd have here together, the lazy weekend afternoons, the workshop full of his stuff, the boat alongside the garage, the lawn

9

decorations and flowers—none of it actually theirs yet—they ended up making love hastily and half-dressed against the wall outside, in the breezeway between the back door and garage. But they did not have enough money, in the end, and they knew it. They were, in most ways, not ready for what they were dreaming as they went at it, that afternoon, against the wall outside. It didn't ruin them, exactly, seeing their application turned down, but for a time it gave what followed in their lives an aura of failure, of having "settled," which played its part in their eventual breakup. Next closest was a recently divorced man, a dentist, who needed the extra space for his children on weekends and school vacations. But, distracted or distraught in his new singleness, he wrote the landlord's name on the inside of a cigarette pack flattened in his date book (he was still pretending, even to himself, that he hadn't started back smoking), lost it or forgot it, and, much to the landlord's surprise, vanished after an hour of solid-seeming discussion only to reappear in another rental property, owned by a friend of the landlord's, several blocks north, still scattered and glum and toying with his new independence, but paying a hundred seventy-five dollars a month less than he would have if he'd rented at 927 West 27th.

The new tenants came with the usual inability to see themselves any more clearly in the future than in the present, and with the usual excitement this can provoke. They had not had sex in at least as many months as the house had stood vacant: there was a dead child involved, but they weren't talking about it anymore—weren't talking, that is, in the sense of searching out new combinations of words and explanations to delineate a cure. The boy would have been a year old. He would have liked the back yard and finished basement for his parties with high school friends and for howling soul-grunge jams erupting into games of Nerf tackle football or kill-the-man-with-the-ball. Mornings, home from college, he would have looked up at her from the breakfast nook over a glass of orange juice in the expectant, desultory manner of her brothers and dead father, and said, "Sure, Ma, I'd eat *any*thing." Always, when they spoke of him or tried imagining the life they'd all three been robbed of the day his umbilical cord tied itself together with her placenta and he came out septic, blue as a gem and dead, they skipped the more immediate scenes—diapers and toys and first teeth, first word, first smile, first tiny nail clippings. They went straight to his older years. It was better that way, they told each other, easier giving him this more familiar figuration, though they weren't sure why—weren't sure it wasn't a perversity or a disgrace. The money from the settlement with the hospital insurance, after lawyers' fees, would go to the mortgage on their old house which they would then put up for rent, offsetting the cost of the new rental exactly. Nothing lost, nothing gained. So, it was a temporary shift, a change of scenery—stop-over, lateral jump—nothing upward or permanent about it; like trading one life-raft for another. The counselor's words for it, when he first introduced the idea months ago, had included phrases like *grief capitulation, reharmonization of the marital space,* and *locus poenitentiae.* In a year or so, they could look again at the situation and decide if they wanted to stay on renting at 927 West 27th, move back across town to the old house and its old sadness and its associations, try to buy the landlord out, or, if it was really for the best, part ways, in which case, the rental would only make it that much easier. They had not fought in their five years of marriage, and they did not fight now. They did not break things, raise their voices, shout, pound fists through plasterboard, or stare vacantly for hours at each other across an unlit room. They discussed.

What she liked best, apart from the breakfast nook with ghosts of her son at various ages drinking orange juice, eyes upturned, awaiting her service—what she enjoyed was being under the house in that finished basement with the pale daylight touching the ceiling through the basement windows, and the thick cream carpet underfoot, and imagining the walls above her holding in place a life she could temporarily step into or out of: the phone ringing, food cooking, TV going, Seamus up there on the phone with friends or clients. She could really see herself here, alone, while all that stuff went on overhead. She'd hole up for hours in the hanging chair and not plan anything, not research new ways of flambéing a steak or salmon, or roasting exotic hors d'oeuvres, finding ways to squeeze more features into a first-class catering event without adding to her cost. She'd just watch the light move across the ceiling, like reflections off a lake, and hear the life going on above her, aside from her, up there. She'd sleep. Read. Be someone else.

Up the narrow, creaking back steps they went, through the kitchen—dim, burnt smells, gas from the range—to the living room, and back again, back down to investigate.

"Perfect place for me to set up shop," she said. "Modem connection there." She pointed. "And I like the light."

"What light?" He breathed in and out next to her. She smelled the cold air trapped in the folds of his overcoat; under that, the smells of his desk sweat and laundered cotton. Tried to remember how that had once pleased her so much—given her such feelings of difference and affection (mixed with some pride at her own tolerance, because really there was something in his smell she never quite liked). Now... what? It didn't drive her from him, but it held her, stricken, immobile, beguiled.

She gestured with her chin toward the ceiling. At the same moment the landlord came into view suddenly, outside, pacing purposefully one way and back again, stopping against the wall where they could see him, legs only, from the mid-thigh down. He bounced on his toes, then stood still—he was one of those heavyset, pin-legged men, always in a hurry, walking tipped forward at the waist as if he couldn't get where he was going fast enough. Wind billowed against his slacks, flattening them to his legs and revealing their exact shape, then gusted up, puffing the pant legs full of frigid air, so he looked like the Michelin man.

It struck her funny. Seamus, too, was laughing—his constricted, close-mouthed laugh. His public laugh. It was one of the things that had drawn her to him, she supposed, six years ago: the sound of that politely friendly, neighing laughter reaching her across the room at the party of a friend of a friend of hers she'd agreed to cater at a bargain. She was twenty-nine then and finished, absolutely done, so she'd say to anyone who asked, with cruel-seeming boy-men whose eyes promised tormenting affection and eventual desertion, and who never failed to deliver on some version of these promises. Whether it was a matter of recurrent bad taste on her part or of a self-fulfilling prophecy and thus self-induced, self-inflicted—some way she drove them from her with the expectation of abandonment, proving herself exactly as unlovable as anticipated (one of them had recently explained it this way for her, which was no help)—hardly mattered. The experiment was done. Lesson learned. Finito. She hadn't been intending to meet Seamus here—hadn't been thinking at all about *guys* or prospective mates; yet there he was: the half-moons of his nails as neat as a doctor's, the sport coat shabby around the cuffs and collar. Tight, youthful jaw line and hair slicked back at the temples, thick black and silver. Nice. Handsome. And that fatherly, neighing laugh. A comfort, an ease about him: it wasn't love or lust at first sight—which was a *good* thing, she'd told herself, given what she'd been drawn to in the past, the trouble she'd gotten herself into always divining mates according to the compass of her libido. She'd liked the sight of him holding her canapé, inserting it whole into his mouth with those big, clean fingers, and biting down. Nodding his head sagely and as if he were offering some mild, fond form of encouragement to the woman he was talking to, absolutely attuned. Then the words, "Yes, yes, that's what I thought," and something else she couldn't catch. She liked the crinkle of laugh wrinkles around his eyes and the flex of his jaw, the sight of him chewing, eyebrows raised, and again that laugh.

Later, as she recounted these first impressions to him, he'd had to set her straight on a few things. The woman she'd seen him talking to was one he'd been set up on a blind date with once, years earlier. "I wasn't *encouraging* her, not exactly. Only to the point that it might help in getting me the hell out of the conversation with a minimum of grief." They hadn't liked or disliked each other, he and this woman, but there was no real chemistry—as far as he was concerned. No spark; almost a nightmare, but not quite. There hadn't been a follow-up date, but he was pretty sure there had been a few unreturned phone calls (his bad) and maybe an embarrassing scene in a grocery store. "Never should have let her touch me. You'd think by then I'd have known better, right? Keep the pants on, keep the zipper up!" But it was a rough, lonely patch in his life; unlucky. Not that he was making excuses. What she'd witnessed that afternoon from across the room at the party of a friend of a friend of hers was the mostly dull and dully uncomfortable fallout of all that: a conversation, tinged with undercurrents of expired wishes for revenge possibly (on the woman's part), and reminders (on his part) of a time in his life he just didn't want to contemplate, much less relive, if he could avoid it. Oddly, he said, he couldn't help having the feeling the woman was still trying to sell herself, if only to prove how undamaged she was. "Maybe that's the thing," he said. "Some people, whatever you say to each other, it feels like a competition. Listing off your boring credentials. You bring that out in each other, maybe because of some way you fundamentally *don't* connect or see the best in one another. Meanwhile, the same person could get on just perfectly with someone else…"

"Like me?" she'd asked.

"Well. You, and a few others."

This was early in their courtship, when one of the main things he'd seemed set on was convincing her of their mutual replaceablility. The myth of the perfect "one and only," he wanted her to know, was just that—a myth. The truth was more like one and several. There were notoriously bad matches, to be sure—but after all the winnowing away, still you'd find there was a surprising number of decent people with whom you could make a life. So, rather than, *You make me happier than I've ever been,* or *You are the best lover in the world for me,* the corrected language went something like, *I feel happy with you,* or *You are certainly as good as anyone I've ever slept with,* etc. How they'd moved on from that, found a middle-ground and agreed to get married after all, she didn't remember exactly. Mainly, she supposed, it had been a matter of capitulation on her part: learning to accept his truth as *the* truth, without necessarily believing it applied to her.

And now here they were, five years later and contemplating the unmaking of all that—contemplating the ruin of a life together, and not even saying so.

"So?"

She nodded. "I think it's good."

"Then let's put the fucker out of his misery." He'd lived in the U.S. almost twenty years; still at times, and most notably when money was involved, he spoke with traces of a Dublin accent. *Fokker.*

"Or we could make him wait. Soften him up a little," she said.

"You're a cruel one. How long? Just the full calendar month, like you did me?"

"I was thinking more like—oh, six-seven minutes. Isn't that what they say, the average for a man, stimulation to climax?" Harmless, empty flirting. Well, maybe not entirely harmless. But harmless enough—he'd know how to take it; know she didn't mean for anything to happen, actually. Too cold here anyway, and who knew what might be on that carpet. She could see him calculating his response now—something to acknowledge her but not too openly, and not dismissively either. Well, and maybe if he was *just* oblique enough, maintaining the little edge of indifference and indirection that made flirting *flirting* after all, combining ardor and opposition exactly the way he used to do to drive her wild, maybe then the little buzz of heat in her womb would work its magic—overwhelm sense to carry her past her usual resistances.

But nothing came—no clever reply. Instead he sighed and moved closer suddenly, stroked her cheek and drew her to him. "Doll," he said. Through his pants and the back of her jacket she felt the press of him, belt buckle, hipbones, pelvis, half-erect penis. Always half-erect. *Penis permanently at half-mast*, he'd tell her, if she asked about it, or commented. For a moment she could almost envision it: the two of them here on the floor, naked, forgetful, engrossed in each other.

Could almost imagine that locked part of herself, the stuck thing in her brain like a window painted shut, suddenly blown open—the obstructed thing just *gone* as easily as whatever was obstructing it. At the back of this imagined scene were some of the counselor's explanations: *Eventually the pathology itself becomes a problem with its own attendant pathologies—call it a ring of meta-pathologies—a whole sub-grouping of resultant neuroses all bearing the fingerprint of the original somewhere in their makeup. All learned. What to do then? Get back to the source of the source of the source, of course!* He was like that. Always talking in aphorisms, Seuss-like rhymes and vague-sounding Latinate scientifications. In a way, now, maybe *he* was the problem, being the speaking embodiment for all that quagmire of thought and reason and emotional excavation. The describer. Good thing they'd be taking a break from their sessions the next little while: their treatment had run its course and now they were onto a possible cure—possible course of action, anyway, with the rental property. Nothing more to say about that, for now. They'd call him again when they were at another turning point. Meanwhile, here was Seamus behind her, one hand cupped over her breast, another pressing her hip, while she was off in head-land rehashing abstractions. How to get away from it?

"There *is* something about this house, though, isn't there?" She pulled herself from him and moved a step away. "It's got this—I don't know what. Energy."

"Yes."

"Feels happy, somehow. A haven. Like things will be *good* here. I feel it—really." She moved another step from him. Reached a hand for his and pressed once firmly, both to promise and to thwart him. Tugged at his coat collar and brushed away some lint. "Let's do it."

"What."

"Put the fucker out of his misery."

He lifted his eyebrows.

"I'm sure of it."

Both of them looked to where the landlord had been standing, but he was gone. Probably back in his car, waiting. Probably already cranking the ignition, cigarette in hand, readying himself for the next defeat, next refusal or deferred response, window open just a crack (strains of Neil Diamond blowing through it with heat from the dashboard vent) to get this over with fast. He'd said not to rush, he was on his lunch, *take your time, make a decision you can live with,* but he was slightly wall-eyed, and the whole time they were talking she couldn't tell where his gaze was fixed—was it the right eye or the left one she should hold in her attention?—and, consequently, she was unsure how to take anything he said. All of it seemed skewed, somehow, toward sarcasm or a weird kind of macho sentimentality. Either one seemed possible. He'd followed them around at first, room to room, slurping Wendy's chili from a styrofoam cup and dabbing at his mouth with a napkin as he pointed out favorite features with his plastic spork, or then stood aside silently watching (or maybe not watching at all, it was hard to say). Ducking out the back door and dropping his lunch remains in the trash, he momentarily convinced her—because of the fastidiousness, the speed and solicitous neatness on display, the intimate knowledge of where everything was—that he must have some ulterior motive, seeing them set up here. Maybe he was a pornographer with hidden cameras planted throughout the house, behind mirrors and inside curtain rods, streaming live video feeds of them straight to the internet. Who could say? No. He was just desperate to rent and trying not to appear so. High-end properties are a bear, he'd said. You need high-end tenants, of which there aren't so damn many in this town, if you catch my drift. Slight limp, she'd thought, but then as he raced ahead of them down the stairs to the basement, the limp was gone. Well, regardless, they'd make him happy. They'd accept his terms—all of them—sign on the line. They were good tenants. Ideal ones, really—any landlord's dream.

THE HOUSE HAD ITS SECRETS: some they came to know, most they didn't. Its doors did not open in every season—some swelled stuck half-open or half-shut and often would not budge without force; some door knobs refused their attachments to the spindle (stripped set-screws, or improperly replaced set-screws) and came off altogether if spun the wrong way, too hard, too fast, leaving you stranded on the wrong side of wherever you wanted to be, severed knob in hand. The floors in the bathrooms concealed generations of dirt and footmarks under layers of tile, linoleum and more linoleum. And there were secret compartments, one opening like a trap in the kitchen floor, another in the bathroom—both designed and constructed by the original owner, a silver mining foreman who'd dabbled weekends as a bootlegger, and both long since sealed away, nailed shut and boarded over. Still, a peculiar, audible hollowness persisted in the flooring—a subtle sinking underfoot, a little extra give, as if an invisible aperture between realities were being crossed unexpectedly. Within one lay the account register for an illicit business (not the bootlegging) long since expired, written in permanent ink, the account itself always a few dollars in the black. In the other a tin containing a woman's lace garter, some matches, several postcard-sized black and whites of a topless girl, the garter stiffened and gone gray from time, the pictures surprisingly well preserved.

Before being a house this had been a marshy stand of ninebark, pine trees, birch, Saskatoon and blueberry bushes, spring-fed, and high enough on the south facing slope of the hill that it was warm well into fall and quick to thaw with each vernal equinox. Once, as part of his vision quest, a boy from the local tribe had spent several days and nights here bivouacked among the trees, alone, waiting and fasting, watching the stars wheel and circle back around again; squirrels, ravens, rabbits, finches, eagles, countless insects came and went. Some larger quadrupeds—often the crackling of branches nearby and a cougar's yowl. His vision consisted of several things, in the end, none of which there are words for in this language. When houses started going up, late nineteenth and early twentieth century—a few hunting shacks and silver miners' mansions, cottages for the help, storage facilities and other outbuildings—the lot stayed mostly as it had always been: dense with overgrowth, notable for its spring-fed marshiness and blueberries, frequented by children playing cowboy and Indian games. For a time, early in the twentieth century, it became criss-crossed with children's trails and was the site, too, for an illicit love triangle involving two young married women and a gypsy. Then came the boom and grids of housing went down, whole neighborhoods superimposed at a single time onto the land—water, septic, electric, all of it at once. The undergrowth was cut then, the spring capped, the land shaved and reshaped, and up went the house. In its core, still, was the capped spring. Two men had died here; three marriages were broken; eighteen children grown to adulthood. Twenty-six makes of car had parked in the garage or on the paved area outside, and two RV's. Nine signed bank notes. Twelve rental agreements. No boats. No one who lived here had ever owned a boat—only the one prospective tenant had dreamed of it, against the south facing wall, and had perhaps been ruined by the dream.

SHE HAD HER SECRETS, TOO—she'd always had. It was what had drawn him to her most irresistibly, he supposed, and what kept him there even now. Her skin: the slight, bruise-like discolorations that showed up where she didn't remember bumping herself or even being touched—forearm, shoulder, hips—purplish marks like smudges under the skin that erupted unaccountably and disappeared just as mysteriously, faded to a dryish patch, absorbed away. The same bruise-like color and texture occasionally manifesting under her eyes, too, regardless of how long or deeply she slept. And the eyes themselves—always absorbing more light than they reflected, brown, doll-like, recalcitrant, vaguely sad even when she was laughing. What did that mean? Her sex, of course, the biggest secret of all—a veritable temple to secrecy, and now indefinitely locked to him. How many times had he touched her in the past—how many times lain between her legs, held her, embraced, touched, tasted every part of her? Now she was altogether off-limits. Now she'd interrupt kissing him to wipe something from her eye or her nose—anxiously shift her weight foot-to-foot, sigh, pat his shoulder as if he were a pony. They still slept as they always had—his feet under hers to warm them, arm across her waist, leg between her legs, hands twined together, nose in her hair. It was mainly for the comfort, he suspected, the habit of comfort, another body to wrap around and sleep enfolded in; there was real intimacy in that, though it never went further. Stopped just short of making the blood sting to the surface of their skin.

He liked watching her dress. Talking with her after dinner and on weekends, occasionally in the bath, he was keenly attuned and watchful. It was the one thing left to satisfy or give him assurance, sexually: the physical evidence of her moving around, fixing her hair, talking on the phone, cutting up vegetables, laughing, etc.; sharing a life. Watching all that. His eyes, he knew, were as insistent and prying as question marks—nothing subtle to it—bent on her everywhere, all his longing and desire displaced into them but never declared outright for fear of further rejection. He was not a man who'd ever cheat.

The new house, the move, the commotion, the energy of packing and unpacking, finding tenants for their house—it should change all this. This was the equation as he had it worked out in his mind, anyway: stasis offset by an outpouring of physical energy, a distraction in labor, followed by renewal. They'd go on as themselves, but altered.

AT FIRST, IT WAS HOW SHE'D PICTURED IT, almost: the light creeping up and steadily across the ceiling, rippling and still like sunlight reflected off a lake, her days alone down here spent mostly letting things go. Letting things slide. There was the daybed with the white metal railing along the back and sides—her mother's, the one she'd died in, the throw blankets she'd knitted and the pillow covers she'd embroidered scattered over it. Across from that, the hanging chair where she could swing and read. Her desk, neat and dusted, pens in cups, papers stacked, sat under the windows, bookshelves beside it lined with cookbooks and three-ring binders for every year of her business, each designated along the spine accordingly, back to 1998. Inside these were the seldom-consulted table diagrams and schedules and food-smeared service plans, recipes, menus, contact names, phone numbers, receipts for down payments, and so on—every last detail. The stuff of her work. Not a thing out of place or gone missing. Sometimes she got up and paced the room thoughtfully, until she heard Seamus's footsteps overhead, at which time she might drop into her desk chair or stick her nose in a magazine and do her best to mock the facial expressions she knew he associated with her most industrious and preoccupied periods of incubation—the looks that told him stay away, I'm busy, I'm working out details on a project, I'm scheming. A few times she even faked conversations on the phone, chomping out numbers and details for imaginary customers or for one of her associates, just to avoid talking. It was the dead season anyway—January, February, March. Nothing much for her to do but mark time until April when people started calling about their weddings and anniversaries and graduation receptions.

Her refusal was partly a deadening. She knew this. A turning in and numbing-up of all her senses. At times she pictured herself like a convection oven gone wrong—the heat blowing in and in, and nothing there to cook or warm. Just this glassy, cross, overheated, blown-dry feeling in her gut, anytime he came too near her and the nerves that had once fired so easily at his touch triggered again, but wrongly. Obversely. Really, she supposed, it was as much a physical thing, biological even, as a psychological one. There might be drugs to help—hormonal supplements (her blood work did not corroborate this, but still). Probably another result of the internal biological havoc so casually referred to as "pregnancy"; a carryover from all that pain and the initial forced abstention following the caesarean—those weeks of cramping, bleeding, stitches in her belly throbbing and tight every way she moved, nipples brown as blood pudding, hard and aching. Foreign to her. All that transformative suffering, none of which he could possibly share. It had become a barrier behind which to hide and keep private the other, deeper pain which she supposed was so much worse because it had no concrete, identifiable source. Nowhere you could point to, put your hand and say, *oww, fucking hell, that hurts, goddamn it*, and then chart its progress back to health again. The pain of his nearness and that physical, emotional distress had become habitual then, she supposed—intertwined into this stuckness and despair, so when the time came that they might have resumed a sex-life it was just easier, right and somehow more satisfying, to keep saying *no*. To keep the barrier up.

Well, it would pass. Or not. For now the *no* felt absolute, nothing tentative about it; like the cutting edge of a shovel going down. There was pain in this for her, too—always refusing—and some relief. Really, it was the only pleasure or relief left for her these days: the pleasure of that meanness and hurt; hurting them both and then holding herself right up against the pain because at least it felt like *something*, refusing him. Like cutting yourself. Once you'd done it and seen yourself bleed a little, you could remember how good it was to be alive.

"You need some new toys, hon." This was Paula, her friend since forever, freshman year of college, on the telephone. In the background a child wailed. One of the twins, probably—the little guys. There were four children: six, and nine, and the twins. It was about all Paula could manage lately, these once- or twice-monthly phone conversations. Carolyne, too; the assault of family noise in the background, always on the verge of chaos, tended to make her ache and feel sick with missing out (some guilty relief, too, at not having actually to endure it herself), in a way that could take days to recover from. "You gotta start by learning to please yourself again, right? That can be a fun time."

"Sure. Maybe so." But she'd tried already, was continually trying, in fact, though not so much with the toys. The buzzing and nasty latex smells just did not appeal. And occasionally (once in recent memory, anyway) she'd managed it, though barely, and never with any reliable set of triggers. How she'd finally stopped *thinking* those times—stopped picturing her vagina as this dead, failed thing, failed project, site for yeast-infections, bleeding, all the rest of it—she was never sure. An essential mystery.

The baby's crying was suddenly much closer, right in her ear and making her nipples tighten unexpectedly—Paula's voice cooing under that (so she must have set the phone in the crib or on an end table or something). A rustling noise—noise of breath—and she was back again. "I mean, maybe it's not really your style, but let me tell you, the wonders of modern technology—they've got some stuff out there to make a girl feel pretty much like a girl all over again. I won't go into details. Suffice to say, sometimes I'm as happy to see Kev on his way out of town as I am to see him home again. Know what I mean?"

"Kevin's a nice guy, Paula. How's business going for him these days?"

"Way to change the subject there."

"I'm just asking."

"Kevin's fine. Got orders coming in left and right on the net. Top seller in his district, if you can believe it. Former slacker turned sales wonder boy. I think it's because of his fortieth coming up, time can be such a motivator, but don't tell him I said that—what…what is it, honey?" Sound of her covering the phone. " —*Not while I'm on the phone. See? When mommy's done talking.*" More rattling and rubbing. "I'm gonna have to cut this one short. Ben says he's got an ear ache. Just trust me on this. I'm buying you a late Christmas present. Be on the lookout for a little brown, unmarked package."

"Nice of you, Paula, but you…"

"Nice is no part of it." A torrent of cries in the background. "Like in a week or two or eight. You tell me if that doesn't fix your wagon."

"What if my *wagon's* not broken?"

"You two will be thanking me for the next twenty years of marriage."

It wouldn't happen. Like the million other empty promises from her, plans made and broken, intended courtesies that never materialized—the visits and trips together, gifts, cards, letters. Family life, she thought. One way or the other, if you had it or if you didn't, it ate you alive, spit you out in a waking dream.

HE DID NOT TELL HER, but the whole dead child thing was beginning to be more and more of a chore. A contrivance and a thing to butt up against in frustration. Overwrought in her in a way he just didn't fathom. His one avenue back into it had been, for a time anyway, holing up in what would have been the boy's bedroom at their old house and watching the flies buzz and skitter against the top pane of the rattly west-facing casement window. The sound of them up there, bumping the glass, and the sunset light distorted and streaky because of how old the glass was, Ponderosa pines outside swinging with the breeze—all of it reminded him; put him back in the frame of mind he'd been anticipating all through her pregnancy—the dilatory, exultant state of mind in which he was a child again and seeing the world anew through his boy's eyes, all its first sights, smells and sounds. Because here by the window was where the boy would have slept; he would have heard those flies and looked up at them, at their mystery in the impossibly tall and mysterious light-streaked windows, and there maybe his hopes of being a famous mountaineer or painter would have begun. He would have heard symphonies in his head, maybe. Poems. Who could say? Seamus would sip his scotch and rock in the little chair meant to be Carolyne's nursing rocker, imagining, and he would wait for the feeling to enter him: the feeling that his perceptions had fused with the lost boy's again; and then the grief that would let him back in with Carolyne. Because really, though he couldn't bring himself to say it to her yet, he was forgetting—ready to move on or try again; displace the longing for progeny elsewhere, maybe, adopt kids, build a boat, work harder to make his mark on the world, something, anything. There was so little time, really. (And maybe that was part of it—the ten years difference between them and how it just bumped him out of things faster; allowed him the necessary perspective or insight: suffering, he might have told her, and would someday, eventually, when the opportunity presented itself, was actually the *norm*, not the exception, as far as he could tell; look at how his own Ma lived and died, whittled away by diabetes; hand-wringing, hair-tearing, what was the use of it, ultimately?) And so, for as long as he could anyway, he forced himself back again and again. Sat in the low rocker, drinking—remembering the day of the loss too, the doors swinging out and the doctor there straight out of ICU, still in her mask and surgical greens, shaking her head before she'd said a word so Seamus had to know, before he knew that he knew, what was coming—until he felt closer again to all that and to what he imagined Carolyne must be feeling. Then he'd return to her, teary-eyed, mouth anesthetized from scotch—only to realize for the umpteenth time that it was no use. His grief was not a comfort for her, it was a torture, the sight of it multiplying her sadness incomprehensibly into rage and driving them ever further apart. Commiseration was just not possible between them. And yet, he thought, if they didn't share grief, soon enough they'd have nothing at all to say to each other.

The new house was different. Here there was no familiar context, no avenue back into the pain. Here he'd see himself in the ancient, rose-tinted bathroom mirror, shaving, feel the flooring bounce and give slightly underfoot as if he were afloat, and he'd know: the pain was going—gone or mostly absorbed. There was about him, now, a general pleasure he couldn't always conceal or control—a little joyousness causing him to whistle and look ahead to things for no good reason. Monday was a *good* day now: happy, back to work. He took it out on the house some too, at night and on weekends. Fixed windowpanes, caulked shower tiling, replaced or tightened doorknob set-screws, spackled and painted walls, repaired wall papering, dusted blinds, scrubbed at the smells of death and patchouli wherever he imagined them to originate, even occasionally moving appliances to get at the years of hidden dirt and debris. He had the sense, too, that he was getting ready for something. Or maybe it was the momentum of all that former expectancy—the habit of that former expectancy still carrying him along. Sure, that might be it: so the loss still went on resounding in him as well, though so differently from the way it did in her. He was alone and expectant, but happily so. And horny as hell. The pan on the stove, more often than not, heating for him alone again—leftovers or old favorite dishes from his bachelor days—the house, the whole upstairs anyway, increasingly his alone, while she sulked downstairs. Mooned away, untouched and untouchable, talking to the lost boy, pretending she didn't know that he knew exactly what she was doing and why, while he, more and more lost to her as well, went about his business.

There was still swimming on Sundays and Wednesday nights, and the occasional walk. Still, sometimes, they'd sit on the couch together with the stereo playing, or the TV. Mindless stuff, mainly, to keep them occupied and side-by-side without having to think or talk. Some nights they were up like that for hours, dreams displaced into the pink and blue junk flickering on the screen at their feet.

KISSING HIM, AT FIRST, had been strange. Not good, not bad. The lips were dry and inward-turning, flexed as if in anticipation of something untoward. She'd wet hers and tried again. "Open slightly. I'll show you," she'd said. And later he'd shared with her the metaphor from his trade that best explained how he felt when she did this. "You use it to describe a breach in the electrical current—when the current goes outside the conduit. It *arcs*. That's how it is for me. Like there's this current arcing out of me and I may be in danger of, like, igniting, if I'm not careful." The dismay, at first, hearing this, and knowing she was in trouble, because she'd been on the opposite side of this equation before—moved nearly to orgasm by kissing a man who'd felt just kind of so-so, take-it-or-leave-it, with her. But then, the realization, hey, it didn't *have* to work like that this time: she was more understanding, by far, than any man she'd ever been with; she could explain things and show Seamus exactly what she liked and how, teach him. And with that, the subsequent burn—the vertigo-like sensations of power and control, themselves an aphrodisiac. So it had improved, and quickly, and soon gone as out of control for her as for him, allowing her to forget those initial misgivings and calculations. Mostly. The current, she supposed, was arcing out of her as well. Racing all over the place, sparks flying everywhere. A virtual romantic cliché.

One night, though, not long before he proposed to her, she'd come over to his apartment late from serving a party—she had her own keys by then and he was asleep. There was always a smell about his place like stale oranges, digested fruit—a heavy flatulent smell just under that, which she'd never considered *his* smell, exactly, but had always thought of as belonging to his apartment or the things in it, and hadn't ever fully registered as repulsive to her. It still wasn't repulsive, exactly, but it held a clue. Made her stop suddenly and think, *no; this is all wrong; I do not love him.* According to her *old* definitions of love, anyway, she didn't. She had to say it out loud: "Seamus McVee, I don't love you and I never have." She was still in the vestibule by his front door, beside the umbrella stand, a hand on his antique coat rack, hearing the pendulum clock tick-tock in the next room, the refrigerator fan suddenly kick on. She wanted to say it again, to test the words—see whether or not she meant them: "I don't love you, Seamus McVee." A giddy, exultant despair, sort of nervous and wrecked, what you'd feel before cutting yourself, because she'd always known this—had known it without trusting herself to allow the knowledge full entry. But then she was remembering the many things she and Seamus always said to each other about willpower and the conscious decision anyone can make to overcome libidinous instinct, to stay together against all odds—how this mattered so much more than any romantic illusions. Remembering, too, all their good times and the ways he was so kind to her, never inattentive, never caught up in himself; his consuming gratitude, too, touching her, even just watching her undress—*that* was a turn-on, among other things, though it was all she could do sometimes not to laugh outright from the guilty pleasure it caused her, and the heady feelings of too much power, as if she were a very spoiled little kid. Then she was picturing his face. *If I told him now*, she thought—*if he knew I didn't love him? Poor thing. Poor Seamus. I couldn't.* She knew first-hand just how *that* would feel. And, after all, she wasn't totally sure of it—only in a fuzzy, intuitive-instinctual kind of way—and if her instincts had taught her one thing by then it was that they were seldom to be trusted, and never where men were concerned. So she'd toed off her work shoes, shed her stinky cook's clothes in the bathroom and dropped them in his laundry hamper, skipped the shower and gone straight to him in the bedroom, straight into that smell that didn't so much repel her as remind her of their difference and of the fact that at some fundamental, intuitive level he just was not the one for her—not the exactly right heart-stopping one. Though for now it didn't matter and she was content not to think about it any further. *I am happy*, she told herself: *I'm as happy as I've ever been and he's as good to me as any man I've known. Better.*

She moistened a fingertip and thought this through again, reliving, remembering some of the earlier, better sensations, skipping the uncertainty. But it was no use. The ache to come spread from her belly but not further, not outward, so touching herself was like touching dead skin—someone else's skin. She peeled away her underwear and rolled onto her side, onto her back again, watched the back of her wrist scribbling madly away. *Now*, she thought. *Now goddamn it. What is wrong with me?* No good. Upstairs she heard the front door open and close, then his footsteps, mail landing on the table, splat, his voice calling for her, announcing he was home. She rolled upright fast and dressed. Zipped, snapped, bloused her top and headed for the bathroom. For a second, glancing up, she thought she caught something moving there in the window—the outline or shadow of a man, a boy, dissolving suddenly, but hovering there still somehow too: dirt-stained knees, feathers, flush-mottled face. A chill and barely comprehensible knowledge came with this, gone the instant it seemed about to surface into language, like the reflection of something in a lake—something she'd dreamed but forgotten.

UPSTAIRS, HE WAS AT THE KITCHEN TABLE, coat on still, flipping through mail, slitting envelopes with a pen knife and setting their contents aside in piles—junk, bills, letters to her. The letters to her, she knew, would all be opened too, slit along the tops, but otherwise untouched—a curatorial, gentlemanly, old-world habit of his (learned from his father, she guessed) she'd found vaguely annoying at first and had eventually come to cherish: saving her the little hassle and risk of paper-cuts, opening her mail. But something was different in him today, his stance or demeanor—she wasn't sure what. He seemed relaxed, buoyant; a man on his way to a party. The shirt was one she didn't recognize—deep pink with a spread collar, perfectly pressed and with a nice visible weave to the fabric. The coat, too—his old black camel hair—the way it hung on him, scooped to the shape of his shoulders, like a sail catching the wind, was unfamiliar somehow; it seemed the embodiment of this *difference*, this indefinable falling away thing or changedness about him. And then it hit her: his grief, however much of it there ever had been, wherever it had come from in him, must no longer be a part of his day-to-day life—no longer something he had to shoulder around. *That* was the difference in him. Those gray weeks and months of mourning he'd held her and endured her silence, her animosity, self-loathing, he'd dropped them off somewhere and gotten on.

"Hey," he said, looked up suddenly. His glasses had slid down and he peered at her over them. "Package for you." He motioned with his chin. "Doesn't say who from."

New haircut, she realized suddenly. That was it. He had a new haircut—new shirt and a haircut. And here she was contemplating this emotional, metaphysical shift for him. The hairdresser, though, had taken particular care shaping the more feverish outgrowths around his temples and sideburns, chopping back and flattening things along the top, so he looked fresh, clean and years younger, handsome and irritatingly sexy.

"That." She waved a hand—felt herself blushing. "From Paula."

He cocked an eyebrow. Smirked. "The long-awaited, uh—gift?"

"Never you mind." She circled the table, fit herself between it and him and slipped into his arms. Reached to remove his eyeglasses and set them on the table behind her with the pen knife. "Just—hold me a sec," she said, but he'd already drawn her in, enfolded her in his arms. He kissed the top of her head, held his mouth there and drew a breath lingeringly.

"Shh," she said. "Don't. Whatever it is you're thinking to say, don't say it." She felt around for his belt loops in the back and locked her fingers through them, pulling slightly.

"But I…"

"Don't. I don't want to know another thing yet." Now it was like a dam had broken in her, that sudden: a flood of heat and wetness just pouring from her, seeping up and up like a hot spring. "Oh," she said. "My. Wow." It was the warmth and hardness of his chest against hers, that simple—or, it could be that simple, anyway, if she let it. "I'm so wet, it's like…what the…?" Then he was lifting her, carrying her, one arm under her ass, the other braced against her back, her legs up around him and straddling his waist. She felt his mouth on her neck and ears, warm, covering her face now, the couch cushions behind her as he eased her down, feet still on the floor, head braced against the back of the couch, and his hands were inside her shirt, pressing, finding the clasp of her bra and releasing it, opening the front buttons to kiss her there and then gently, and with the unnerving detachment she'd always found so tantalizing, so pleasingly *deliberate*, whisked open her fly and the clasp of her pants, lifted and skinned her out of them that fast, kissing her everywhere—no part of her immune to it anymore: thighs, knees, belly, calves, thighs again, then parting her legs and he was right on it, his tongue inside her, drawing her out of herself so fast, so hard, she could hardly breathe for coming. "OK—OK. Fuck. Jesus Christ. Wait…" She had to stop him. "I can't…" Grabbed his hair and drew him up to her—his mouth on hers, tasting of her, a little soapy, a little like beer.

"Oh my God. Before you came home, I was just," she laughed, "I was trying, you know to make myself come? Ha! No luck, of course. But I must have, like—something must have unlocked in there because man oh man that was just completely unreal…"

"You know what they say, abstinence makes the hard-on fonder."

"Makes the hard-on wander, more like."

"That too. But never this one."

"But honey," she said. He was inside her now, slipping, rocking himself in and out, her thighs braced against his forearms—again that unnerving deliberation, that poise about him, like he was calculating a golf shot. "It doesn't change anything. Right? Because we're having sex—it doesn't change anything. We're still the same—right where we were, and I don't know what—don't know that means but—if we go back home now, or what…"

Now it was his turn to *shush* her. He covered her mouth with a hand; pressed until she felt his ring on her lip and tasted blood. Then his mouth on hers again, breath flooding her lungs.

"No talking," he said. "Right?"

Thrashed her head back and forth. "Unless I have to say something."

He leaned away from her, reared back, lifted her hips to join his. His shirt was halfway unbuttoned and his coat gone (when had that happened? Was it all that much of a blur? Apparently so), collar rumpled, gelled hair sticking up comb-like in disparate, serrated ridges. "Look," he said, gesturing. Sunlight sparkled on the parquet-tiled floor, in the glass in the windows, on every surface—russet, lemon, coming in prismatic bursts through the beveled edges of the dividing lights in the west facing window. "You made the sun come out."

"I have no such powers."

"Don't," he said. "Don't move." He pinned her hips with his hands; stilled himself, too, pulsing, immobile inside her. "I'm right on the edge. I want this to last."

"Don't hold back."

"A little late for that, don't you think? Here I've been holding…"

"Oh don't—! Don't wreck it!"

He fell onto her laughing—both of them laughing—and she seized him; drew him in, pressing with fingernails and the tips of her fingers so he could not move; pressed and didn't let go until there was that jump and sudden release, his whole body tensed laterally as if for a strike and then the gasp and breath out and the throbbing there where her fingers pressed him, the pulsations that always reminded her somehow of drinking or being drunken.

HE'D COME TO SEE about the doorknob set-screws and about a leaky faucet in the basement bathroom. Hadn't wanted to bother them on a Friday evening, but what the heck. It was his only free time this week and wouldn't take long; then he'd be done, the weekend all his. Well, but a landlord's work is never *done,* really. No saying what the weekend would bring.

As always, showing up at this property he had the same conflicting feelings of worry, doubt, astonished pride, and terror. This house was such a bloodsucker *and* such a beauty, with its sweetly pointed tri-tone brick and soaring gables, dividing-lights in the front picture windows, three-tone paint job matching the brick, and old fashioned cedar shake roof. It needed so much *work.* Look how it had already appreciated though, something like thirty thousand in the decade since he'd bought it; if you trusted the current market trends and lending rates, as most people did, with a little better than average maintenance he could sell it in another ten years for a breathtaking profit. Put his daughter through college. That was the plan anyway. House equals Belinda's future. The whole freaking rest of Belinda's *life*—think about *that* for a second. But what a drain, what a bloodsucker. All fall and half the winter sitting there vacant, dust bunnies chasing around the haunted floors, squirrels in the eaves (again), breezes through the fucked-up window casings, washers in every sink and spigot corroding away from disuse. What a waste. If he was smart, really smart, what he'd do is sell off those other properties, the duplexes, further down the ridge—that'd be the smart thing; sell those crappy duplexes, pay down the mortgage here and just sock away every extra rental dollar. Buy stock maybe. The town was growing. He'd make a killing when he sold it. Why then—why didn't he? It was something unspecific about the house itself that worried him: beautiful and functional as it was, it had this aura of doom. Terrified him. What if it didn't rent? Why, for instance, did no one *ever* stay here more than a year, and then why did it always sit empty for so goddamn many months? Made no sense. Perfect location for a bunch of grad students, young married couple with kids. No, fuck the students. The kids too. He didn't *want* any students or young kids with dogs and cats fucking up the inside of his baby. This baby was his daughter's college tuition right here. This was her future—the whole rest of her life. So he kept the duplexes as a hedge against whatever it was that freaked him out about 927 West 27th, spread the mortgage payments between his properties and got by. Always, just barely, got by.

Up the back walkway he came, fumbling with the wad of his keys—the Schlage with the bit of duct tape on the hilt out now, ready to stab into the lock and turn. They weren't home; he was sure of it. Hadn't called, but hadn't seen a car in the drive or parked out front either. No lights on inside. Probably off somewhere together—out at the symphony. Dinner, then the symphony. People like them probably would go to the symphony. Well, best to knock or ring once first anyway, just as a precaution. There was that friend of his, Benny, barged in on a drug deal going down in one of his rental properties—there to unplug a septic line—and got himself blasted in the shoulder a few times instead. Spent months in a sling. Lucky he wasn't shot dead.

Now something had caught his eye. He hadn't rung yet or coughed or whistled or made any of the other friendly preemptory advance-warning I'm-on-my-way-inside-now noises that always consciously or unconsciously preceded his entry into an occupied property. A flash of flesh down there in the basement window. Flash of bare leg and pubic hair. Oh. This was the sort of thing you always hoped for and dreamed about, at the same time you counted yourself lucky that it would never *actually* happen because of the trouble it would get you in. That woman who rented here, too—she was pretty hot, if he remembered right. Gloomy as hell and kind of stiff, like she needed a good smack in the ass or whatever, but definitely a looker. Nice tits and that prim uptight look about her, a little bitchy. What was it she said to him that day—something about a type of cooking oil that had a high smoke-point? The notion of there being different oils and ways of using them, different temperatures they could cook at—he'd liked that. It was a habit of his, collecting bits of obscure but useful information on subjects he'd never thought to wonder about before, like that—grapeseed oil, that was it…

But what the *hell* was she doing?

He had to see this a little better. Gripping the handrail for balance, he leaned as far to the side as he could and looked down— in. There was a smell of wood smoke in the air, blown toward him and away again, food cooking somewhere up the street too, smelled like a meatloaf.

It was her all right. Naked as…well, from the waist down anyway, naked as any centerfold, and pretty well getting off on her own. Flipping around side to side and watching herself do it.

If he was smart he'd get the hell out of here, and fast. He didn't need any lawsuits. This was her private business, and obviously nothing for him to look at. What was the world coming to these days, anyway—people always spying on each other with cameras and webcams, sometimes paying each other for it, sometimes not. Reality

TV. Did he really want to be a part of that sickness? What if it was *his* girl down there—his Belinda? What if he were some loony fuck spying on *her*?

But he wasn't, and this wasn't Belinda. And anyway, he wouldn't look long.

Quietly, he set his bucket with the pipe wrenches and mop sponge on the landing behind him and squatted onto his heels. One little peek, that was it. Then he'd be on his way. Call her on the cellphone in a while and give her a few minutes to put herself back together.

But he didn't think she'd look right back up at him—didn't think she'd shutter her eyelids like she was winking, and didn't think that'd unnerve him so much his throat would suddenly close and he'd be too stunned to move. This was like a vision—like something he'd dreamed without even knowing he was dreaming it, so pretty and perfect and solitary, the white of her legs opened like that and the perfect smudge of her hair, her hand darting in and out, veins showing in the shiny skin of her forehead.

Car door slamming out front.

Fuck.

He lurched backward and upright.

Stood hunched, hands on his knees like a lineman, breathing hard, erection stuck in the folds of his jeans.

Next, the sound of the front door, the key in it turning, hinges creaking. The man; home from work late; he was inside now, saying something—calling out for her. And there she was now—he leaned to see it—also suddenly upright and pulling on her clothes, sniffing her fingertips, looking right at him again and fluffing her hair, straightening her hair around her face. Looking again at him, then turning suddenly and fleeing out of sight, upstairs. What? She hadn't seen him after all? Seen something else in the glass, maybe—some kind of spook or shadow? He stood straight. Leaned again to peer quickly inside. Nothing. Good. Grab the bucket—get the fuck out of here before one of them decides to have a little stroll out the back door. Those set-screws, the leaky faucet, they could wait.

He stole quietly back up the walkway and into his truck.

Still, it lay like a bandage over his brain, this picture of her, obliterating sight—her hand, her legs open, the look on her face, rapt, astonished, and the way she threw her head back, staring right at him. For days afterward it was like that: a thing he couldn't shake, and kept referring back to in his thoughts—kept seeing just under the surface anywhere he looked, in other women's faces, fingers and flesh—until it was so thoroughly a part of his own interior life it was like it hadn't involved her at all. So, by the time she called, a month or two later, to talk about breaking out of their lease, he'd almost forgotten—almost forgotten this was *her*, and found he could talk to her like any woman he hadn't happened to witness with her pants off, in climax. He was in a bad mood, anyway, for reasons relating to one of his other tenants, gambling debts, and a recent flare-up of the old knee injuries from high school football days, ready to take it out on someone. "Lady," he said, "You're calling me to say you want out of a legal document you signed of your own free will with your husband six months ago? I'm not in the habit of breaking my legal agreements, are you?" This wasn't right—he should be nicer. He remembered the months the house had stood empty; saw her down there again, alone in the basement. "You think I'm making exceptions for you because you've suffered some kind of 'emotional trauma'? You think I make a habit of bankrolling other peoples' emotional problems? I got bills to pay—got a business to run. You must be dreaming."

HAPPY FOR YOU

FOR THE MOMENT, she is asleep—an ethereal gray sleep, something like the color of brain matter or of wet cement at dawn, or of the light seeping across her ceiling. A window fan at the foot of her bed whisks air into the room—wet, early spring air—furls and unfurls it around her, keeping her aloft in dreams. She remains oblivious to her snores, her frizzy, gray-black hair threaded with white, some caught in the straps of her nightgown, her freckled shoulders and forearms exposed where she's thrown down the bedding, her pouty, bow-tie shaped mouth—faint tissue-paper wrinkles around the lips—slack and pushed open from sleep. The eyebrows she has from her father. They are straight and dark, nearly connecting at the center, and communicative in ways she doesn't always control or intend, outlining her eyes and giving her expressions a seriousness that offsets the mouth's mostly unintended sensuality. The mouth is a genetic fluke, a slip in time back to her maternal grandmother's mother (turn-of-the-century, silver-town bordello queen). No one else in the family has ever had one like it or ever will.

The phone rings, jerking her from this gray ethereality, aches in her joints and muscles all previously dissolved out of reason magically reasserting themselves. Pieces of earlier dreams resurrect and fade again as the summons persists—bits of hacked up corpse on blood-slick cement; a seaside house consumed in smoke and flames; a woman in a wicker wheelchair waiting at the top of a cliff somewhere near the house, perhaps about to be flung to her untimely death. No matter. She's used to all this. She's been having these dreams for years now, so long she's almost ready to count them an unalterable part of her psyche, like the mouth and eyebrows, in a way—genetically coded or predestined and always causing the odd corona of unintended aftereffect to surround so many of her thoughts and public interactions.

The phone. It's still shrieking. Where the...? She reaches, finds it, eyes still shut, grabs and draws it toward her. But the cord is tangled somewhere and the phone base smashes to the floor—crash-ring—handset slipping from her grip after it with a secondary thumping noise, into the skeins of colored dust under the bed. And now she's really awake, out of bed, stomping around, grabbing the pieces up separately, shouting into the one:

"Hello? Hello?" Heart racing. Thinking: *Who this time? Who's dying?*

She peers through the dark at the caller ID thing on the nightstand which her older son, the airline pilot, bought for her last month (thus the shortened, tangled cord) and helped her to set up. But it's too dark—light still netted and shadowy, like being under water—and she knows this, though knowing doesn't stop her from straining, at least a little, to make out the numbers in the display; see who's calling at such an hour like this, and brace herself for unexpected news.

"Hi there! It's me."

Ben. Her younger son. Now in year five of his PhD studies in neurobiology at the university back East, and living with that hunk of a lab tech and their two great Pyrenees. The dogs she can't stand. The lab tech is another matter. All abs and no brains, she likes saying. Ben will eventually do better, she guesses, find someone more ambitious, educated, culturally attuned, more accepting of his needs and peculiarities. Meanwhile, why shouldn't he enjoy himself? More than once, visiting, she's caught herself gazing after the boyfriend and wondering how her son managed to select a partner who so perfectly embodies her *own* male ideal of years past—her own perfect "himbo," as Ben might put it. How did that little piece of genetic detritus pass to him, and so intact?"

"Ben," he continues, apparently taking her silence for something other than sleepy-headedness. "Your son."

"Yes. But why—what's going on? Is everything OK?"

Silence at the other end of the line. Static, breathing noises. Then, "I dunno. Nothing much. I got up early and had this crazy urge..."

"Brain-o—do you have any idea what time it is?"

"What time..." Sound of him slapping himself in the forehead or bumping the phone against the heel of his hand. "Oh, I am such a loser." More thumping. "Three hours *earlier* out there. How do I always forget?"

The impulse to call him what he is—impossible, continually self-dramatizing, dreamy—competes briefly with the urge to crush him to her, tell him everything's OK, and love him a little harder, a little more unmistakably.

"It's fine. just give me a second to collect myself." Yawn until ears pop, eyes water, jaw feels practically unhinged; pull the old net of consciousness back around her, stretched to the four corners of reason. It's familiar—so familiar, this half-conscious state of alarm. What is it she's reminded of? Something she was dreaming? No. Further out, back in the past. Whatever. She'll remember, or she won't. "I was sound asleep. And you're sure everything's good... everything's all right there?"

"Oh, it's all *fine,* mostly. Fantastic." How he manages to do that, modulate so quickly to a tone of voice which is cheerful and off-puttingly sarcastic, giving nothing away, has always been beyond her. She has to guard against her own reactions to it, her tendency to be provoked and prickly back, rather than letting him know how glad she is to hear his voice whenever, any time of day or night. "Actually, it's kind of embarrassing, what I was calling for. You should forget it.

Go on back to sleep. I can call again in a few hours."

"No. I'm up now, you may as well do me the honor."

"It's OK. Why don't we just…"

"I'll have to buy you one of those fancy Hammacher Schlemmer clocks, you know, with the multiple time zones. Boston, Paris, and Winters, California, so you can always…"

"Mom. I said I was sorry."

"I didn't catch that part…"

"Well, I am. I'm sorry, Ma." But he doesn't sound it, really—probably because of the way she's razzing him. Or because of what comes next (sheepishly, quietly, almost without the usual reserve of sarcasm): "I wanted…I was calling because I was wondering if you could give me the recipe for your Easter bunny-meringue things. That and the egg thingamies you used to make for us. You know—the peanut butter, date glob things with the little bits of fruit?"

"Apricots?"

"Apricots. Right. And your roast and the Jell-O salad with marshmallows—while we're at it."

"You woke me up to talk about dates and bunny meringues."

"Well, I told you it was stupid and could wait! The thing is, I'm making baskets—a basket for Damien. The whole deal. He thinks it's just silly kid stuff, my reminiscences about Michael and I growing up—Easter mornings with you and Michael, whatever. So, I just wanted to show him—do it like the way you used to for us, so he can see what I'm talking about. Like—a shared frame of reference thing?"

"Well…" Again the competing urges: one to look beneath the impossible treacliness of this request, the sentimentality of it, and maybe sniff out some deeper source; the other to throw herself in alongside him, remembering it all—to give him everything he says he wants. More. "Well, you're kind of late getting started, for one thing. I used to be up half the night before, baking and assembling yours. The meringues can be pesky as hell. Do you have baking parchment?"

"No, but that's a can-do. I've got the day off and they're not arriving here until like just before dinner. OK, I'm making a list. *Baking parchment*."

They? The word slips past her. Almost. Sticks and then slips past. Ticks off a vague worry.

Now she's gone, back beyond her dreams to their inadvertent cause maybe, one of them anyway, remembering through feeling: those years and years of being nothing, no one at all, just *Mom*. Sometimes Mother, Ma; occasionally in rage or frustration the verbal equivalent of a one-note jazz solo, the single syllable stretched to suit as many emotions and longings as necessary: *Mah*-ah-ah-*ahh*-ah*M*m. Source and resource. The woman behind the screen and at the same time holding the screen up, cleaning, cooking, organizing, tidying, instigating—daily creating this myth for them to believe in: the world as an ordered place with boys' toys belonging on certain shelves and outgrown clothes sorted into boxes in the basement, a sequence of grades to evolve through and important dates, accomplishments, school holidays, letters to father, honor rolls, and a specified consequence for every misdeed. The blank screen of her former self (really it's more like a rack or a set of dusty shelves than a screen) onto which her action dreams are projected now? Her self of the past stranded in a wicker wheelchair and about to be flung down to its death? Well, it's as likely as the next interpretation, if anything means anything at all.

With this comes a picture, blurred and made general by its repetition, annually: her, alone, late night. Sense of cold emanating through walls and darkness outside the windows; smells of gas, cooking sugar and egg, burnt oven-spill, music up loud but not too loud (her favorites then—Jefferson Airplane or The Moody Blues), and the exhaustion through her hips as she shifts weight foot to foot; the mess of crumbled meringues everywhere, coconut shavings, bits of cut-up paper from half-finished pop-up cards, fake grass from the baskets, and her own hands down there—hers really? What are they doing? Why?—deftly shaping whipped whites into birds, angels, rabbits. Deftly spooning each one onto the tray, or then later peeling them back from the parchment, gooey and burnt underneath, and that feeling in her solar plexus as the damn things resist, refuse her, stick, and finally *un*stick—a giddy, uneven hunger and a longing for this to be done (excitement, too, at the thought of their faces in the morning, fooled again). But they were not fussy kids—they would have been satisfied with just about anything. Run to the corner grocery for a generic, shrink-wrapped basket of jelly beans and chocolate eggs. They wouldn't have minded, might not have noticed at all. Why the extra effort, everything made by hand? The answer is in her, not them, she knows, but it's tricky to get at—too much entangled with all her old mothering habits and the urge to take on everything at once, regardless of the cost.

"You'll want to start with the bunny meringues, and while they're baking and cooling you can do the peanut butter eggs, and pop-up cards if you're feeling really ambitious." Silence. "You'll need recipes for all of this, right?"

Pause. "If it's not too much trouble. Well, I could look online, at least for the ham, and the Jell-O salad…"

"Oh, no. No point my tossing and turning the rest of the morning waiting for the buzzer to go. You know me—once I'm up, I'm up. Better living through chemistry, as I always say." Meaning: *Advil, extra coffee, chocolate, I'll be all right.* She's groping for her bathrobe, shrugging it on, then her slippers, sipping from the glass of tepid water at her bedside, pausing a moment to assess the pressure in her bladder. OK for now. "But you'll have to give me a sec. God knows where all those old things have got to."

This is not the truth. Not only does she know exactly where all her index cards with the old-time kids' favorite recipes are filed *(just in case either of them was ever to change his mind and decide to have children, after all—they'd be here, right to hand)*, she can picture each one so vividly—the food stains, fingerprints, and miscellaneous smears, and her own crimped handwriting, the permanent-ink drawings of angels' wings and rabbits' footprints she'd done in every blank space and corner, out of boredom or affection or sugar-high late-night delirium (she could hardly tell the difference then)—she could probably recite everything he's asking for from memory, start to finish, including ingredients, amounts, temperatures, baking times, stove-top cooking times, and tips for turning things out exactly right. But this little deceit will keep him with her on the phone longer. Also, it presents the image of her she'd most like him to have right now: detached and forgetful, but happily so; freed and solitary rather than alone or jettisoned, and done with all the childhood stuff. A woman-person, not *Mom,* and no longer guardian of his past.

They. The word is there still—a splinter in the mind to feel without exactly thinking of it.

"Hang on two secs," she says—drops the phone on her pillow, ducks down the hall for the newer cordless and back again to beep the one on and hang up the other. "Back again."

"Hi."

"And how is Damien?"

"Oh, fine. He's fine." His voice is different in this phone, nearer and staticky, more obviously digitized, like he's been squashed flat, but closer, right in her ear. There's another quality of sarcasm in it, too, one she's mistaken often enough in the past so that now she braces herself intuitively—a kind of sullenness which usually signals emotional trouble just on the horizon, some pain barely withheld revealing itself first as prickliness. "That cycling club he's in? They signed him up to lead a century ride next weekend, so he's out training with some of the guys now—running some of the route. It's like an hour drive each way, and then a ride of what, like, two, three hours. They're doing the last part of the route today. Forty, fifty miles, something like that. You should see, though, his thighs—I mean, if you thought *before* he was pretty buff?"

"When did I ever say that?"

He's laughing now—sibilant, raucous. The laugh she associates with his early teenage years and that she'd first thought of as an affectation, and has since come to consider one of the final vestiges of his carefree, childhood self. With this comes another picture: the cuffs and collars of his shirts—T-shirts, jerseys, sweaters, every shirt he'd worn through his middle school years—always stretched out of shape and shredded with bite marks because he could not stop himself from sucking and chewing on the threads. That shape, the specific eaten-in curvature of his collars and cuffs and sleeves, always seeming to her a rebuke or a sign maybe, an outward display of something he needed but had no words for.

"Only all the *time*, Ma. You really—you don't remember?"

"Well, maybe once or twice." She flips on lights and flips them out again behind her as she goes room to room, down the three steps and through the sunken living room, its shag rug and tall oak furniture, the mahogany sideboard, then up again into the hallway and through that to the kitchen. "So, tell me—what else…?" she begins, but he is already speaking.

"There's another thing, one other thing I wanted…needed to talk to you about—besides the baskets and the dinner."

Feet stop, heart stops, stomach flip-flops. That tone of voice— the one she will never completely get over and never completely forgive him for, never get used to—the one he's always using to announce his surprises and uncover his own longstanding deceits: *Ma, I'm not coming home for Christmas at all; I haven't gone to any of my classes since the start of the year now—I'm actually not at Vassar, I'm in Europe; no, I'm not getting married to Charmaine after all; she isn't pregnant; terminated; no, Ma, listen, I'm gay.* Always on the phone. Half their relationship since he finished high school—no, more than that, seventy, eighty percent—has taken place on the telephone. She's bent herself to it like a bat, sounding him out with her own shifty mixture of cajoling, irascibility, and love. Hand on the rheostat at the kitchen door now, she has words ready for any number of eventualities (ones she'd probably never use, but rehearses all the same): *Don't tell me—AIDS? You think you're going to beat me to the grave? Blew your teaching stipend on another cashmere sweater and now you need help getting to the end of the month? Ask him, ask your father then. Enough is enough.* She had not, unlike those other mothers she'd gotten to know and consulted with, briefly, however many years ago it was now when he first "came out" and she needed the support, always *known*. There had been no early, outward sign, no unequivocal proclamation. To hear him tell it, it was something he'd evolved to, trial and error, without much sense of its inevitability until the end. As far as she was concerned, it was a thunderbolt out of the blue.

"Yes?"

He still isn't saying anything.

"Well?"

"Just… OK you should know, *he's* coming too."

"*He* who? And where's he coming?"

"Dad."

"Your… You're… What?" Pause. "After how many years?"

"That's right. Bringing the little one and his, uh—the latest wife. For dinner. Kind of a shocker, though, isn't it? Which is another reason I thought I'd do the whole Easter deal. Preserve family tradition, you know? A basket for each of us. Egg hunt to follow. Of course, I mean, I know I'll never do it justice, the way you could, but the gesture, I thought it'd bring it all back around for him, maybe keep things from going too far off track…"

Now she understands. The time confusion, that odd tone of voice, the effort to conceal. Of course. For him this is a *very big deal*. He and Tad have not been face-to-face in years. Four or five, at least. Maybe more. Blood surges again, a tick too quickly, carrying her just past anger to a familiar kind of defeat and self-dislike. She knows the symptoms. Knows, too, how she'll just *burn*, later on, when the anger does come, picturing them all around the table at Ben's house, enjoying one another's company and eating *her* dishes, *her* bunny- and angel-meringue cookies and roast and Jell-O salad. And how he'd brought it out to her, too, with such delicacy, such ostentatiously delicate restraint. As if she needed his protection (and from what? What is she to him, some loony, jealous virago?). All this she knows, but none of it comes to words. Her eyebrows stay straight and serene, her mouth like the love-thoughts of men from a prior century. To see her, you wouldn't guess the racket of feeling and abrupt awareness occurring within.

"How nice for you."

"We've been in touch some recently, Ma. You know that. *Mending fences*, as it were."

"Well, and I guess now I'm supposed to tell you how sorry I am I can't be there—and…"

"Puh-lease!" A different sort of laugh, here. One she likes a lot less. Dismissive, manly. "You wouldn't touch it with a ten-foot pole, Ma."

"If the pole had a sharp point at the end of it, I might…"

Bursts of laughter. "Poisoned, of course."

"No, just the point, I think—thrown from short range—but that's nothing against you or Damien, I hope you understand."

Another memory—one that haunts her at least daily, and which he could not possibly know anything about, unless she were to tell him: pre-courtship, just after college and birding with Tad at UC Davis. It's so vivid, so poignant, even now, part of her wants to believe it must still be back there—the exact moment, the original *frisson* of smell and sight and the texture of the air—all of it perfectly intact. If she could just get back there somehow, maybe visit…but no, she's *been* back a few times and walked those same plank gangways along the estuary of the American River where the new concrete subdivisions went up in the late eighties and then the dot-com boom mansions of the nineties. She knows it's all gone now. *You never cross the same river twice,* as her dad always said. Yet the feeling persists. On view that day were two species of birds rare for California—one, a clan of migratory cranes, the other a type of pileated woodpecker no one ever got a good enough look at to be sure it was really there. The cranes they'd happily tracked for hours, she and a sextet of similarly khaki-clad and tripod-toting birders. She knew the man beside her in his safari shirt with mesh pockets and cane hat (sweat beading through the rim of it) only slightly, but already she had the sense that he was someone she might care for. She knew it from the way he carried himself and from his general demeanor, genial and combative (also, something in her that felt pricked by that, challenged to argument but without all the usual rancor)—in the same way she knew, each time she dipped her eyes to the glass of her binoculars and spun the lenses to focus, that the cranes would be right there, right where *she* was looking (she had the touch that day), in the distance, unaware, going about their business: the emblem at the end of the emblematic search, standing there serenely up to their ankles in muck, eating, indifferent. Preening. Fishing up another mouthful from the muck. Flapping a little further on. She'd met him a few times already—in fact, they'd been crossing paths for months without exchanging more than a few words, at the grocery store, gas station, movie theater. They were neighbors, practically, though in a neighborhood where this meant little or nothing at all, until that day. Driving to meet the rest of the birding club for his first time he'd sat on his eyeglasses, snapping them at the bridge and crushing one of the lenses. He could still manage to see, for the most part—he'd hold the remaining lens to an eye, upside-down, and focus the binoculars with his free hand—but it wasn't easy. All afternoon he was asking her to describe again for him, in a whisper, where to look; where the cranes were, and what they were doing. "Eureka. You're an angel! Be my eyes. *Be thou mine eyes!* Note the compact plumage, schizognathous skull, elevated hind toe…heh! Who ever said they were like herons? The nostrils, particularly on that one—oh. No, he just—where'd he go?" It was like that. They'd known, both of them, on the spot, that there was this fit, something just comfortable and congruous about their efforts together—or, it was easy enough to decide afterward, anyway, that they'd known. The sun was hot as a hand down the back of her shirt, drawing down the sweat from her hair into the waistband of her shorts.

With the lights up full it's still dark enough outside that she sees herself reflected in the kitchen window. She is surprised at the image (*I'm that young still? That old? That faded and vague already?*), and for a moment she wonders if this isn't exactly how she'll appear later, dead and on the haunt (if she continues that way, as a ghost, which she highly doubts, never having seen one), just this streaky, and eerily misshapen. Herself at all ages. She supposes the worst, most painful part of coming face-to-face with an illuminating God or creator (if such a One exists) would be recognizing, finally, her own lifelong loneliness and anguish in isolation from Him (lifelong infidelity forged in foolishness?)—feeling that one last time, too, as it was taken from her. Maybe something like the way she felt just after the boys left home the last time and she understood how the rest of her days were now hers alone to fill. The panic and feelings of nervous distraction—and the gradual sublimation of these unsettled responses into work. Study. Not just birds after all, but their mammalian counterparts, too—most perfectly aerial of all animals and the only mammals capable of true flight. Chiroptera. Back beyond the image of her floating in the glass is that other thing, too—the other imagined life she's always dreaming where it's all bloodshed and espionage, heart-racing urgency.

"Brain-o," she says. His childhood nickname. The second time she's used it in the conversation so far. It'll bring him back right to where she's always claiming to herself she no longer wants him. "I'm just...I don't know what to say. He's your father, I guess. You should know him. It's a good thing. You should be friends. On friendlier terms, that is. But just...watch your feelings. Please. We don't need another breakdown..."

"Exactly. You think I'm not thinking? And the best way to keep him from ever having that kind of effect is to face him straight on. Confront the proverbial bear in his den—to steal a page from your book. Watch the bear, but don't poke the bear with a stick. Have a good look around and see how things are with the bear, but leave him right where you found him."

Suddenly, she sees that she's crying. There's the shine of it on her cheeks, reflected in the glass. She hadn't realized she was this close, though it isn't exactly a surprise, either. Because no matter what Tad does—no matter how many months and years he goes without calling or visiting, never acknowledging how the boys have gotten on in their lives; no matter how much of her *own* life he's robbed and given nothing in exchange for—the moment he resurfaces, it's always the same. Stop everything, call Mom to tell her about it, put on a show, cook him a feast, spare no effort anticipating his every wish. It goes beyond infuriating, it's so unjust and illogical. *I'm happy for you,* she wants to say. Can feel the words in her throat, almost. Can't quite get to them, though. *So glad there's this opening for you again with your father. It'll be good. It'll be fine. All these years, and it's meant so much to you.* No matter how many times she comes to this realization, knowing all over again that what's lost can never be *un*lost, and that there is in her, still, this reservoir of undiminishing bitterness never to be equaled by anything she knows of, save her love for the boys— no matter how many times she recognizes that she already knows all this, it always brings her to tears.

No. Time to back up a little. Raise the defenses. "And would you like to know—what I've been up to? How I plan to spend *my* Easter?"

"You told me before, Ma. The last time we were talking. You and your friends from the library. You're meeting for a potluck and a walk in the park. Right? Unless you've changed plans."

"Yes, and afterwards I thought I might jump off a cliff or small hill or something."

"Mother." Nervous chuckle. "You're not jumping off any cliffs. There *aren't* any cliffs where you live—not in walking distance."

"Well, maybe I could just throw myself under a railroad car instead."

"Not funny, Ma. Can you hear how hard I'm not laughing? Say you understand what you're saying, Mother."

"You understand what you're saying."

"Jesus."

"Anyway, I didn't say the railroad car would be *moving*, did I? Listen, kid." She has to say this. All of it. True, it's out of character for her and nothing he probably wants very much to hear, but she can't stop herself. "Listen. When we were younger we thought it was, like...I did anyway, like there was this kink in my soul. This flaw type of a thing...I don't know what to call it...this *crack* which normal people probably didn't have. Anyway it was something you knew you'd eventually fix or be rid of it—outgrow it, for sure—fill it in, probably by finding someone to give you children, make you complete and happy. Because, essentially, what we believed then, if we believed anything, was that we could be or should be *perfect*. I guess I'm talking about loneliness and despair now, honey. Death. The fear of it anyway. You know—that feeling in the middle of the night when you wake up and can't think of a single good excuse for your existence? But the truth is, honey, it's not a crack or a mistake, it's not an imperfection, or a misperception, and it's not a temporary state either, and it's not your fault and it never goes away. No point fighting. It's *you*. It's life. And even after you start realizing, you can go for years wishing it away—stay busy in your day-to-day life. But at some point it catches up again and you have to begin facing facts. You start losing everyone you ever loved—everything you thought you cared about. One after another, gone. Boom. Everyone drifts away or dies or stops talking to you. Everything you thought *mattered* so much. What's the point? What was the point of all that? And honey the main thing here is...I want you to know how sorry I am that we didn't do a little better by you—didn't protect you from our failures and shortcomings as people. We let ourselves get in the way of being better parents for you, I'm afraid."

Silence. Has he heard her? Did she really just say all that?

"Well, and that about wraps up *this* year's edition of *cheerful Easter morning thoughts from Mom*," he says, mock radio-announcer style. "Remember folks, just because you *are* one or don't *have* one anymore, or don't think you have any use for them, generally, it doesn't mean you shouldn't still listen to *my* mom. She knows *everything*. Next up, why African nations shouldn't have their own systems of governance. No, don't send us money—we wouldn't know what to do with it! You know what? Buy yourselves a dildo instead and have a good time."

So unfair! The thing about dildos, she'd blurted it out to him years ago, in the midst of one of her own awakenings, learning how to get by in the world of AIDS and rampant STDs without a regular partner—practical, big-sisterish advice tinged with comradely bitterness. Cruel of him, taking a remark like that so out of context, turning it against her this way. Same with the African nations comment; of course she hadn't been serious. For a young man with such a consuming sense of the ironic, he seems to her, at times, pathologically unattuned to anyone else's sarcasm (hers, especially). Perhaps this is the root of *all* their trouble, why they can't ever seem to understand each other fully.

"That isn't what I was saying."

"No, true—you didn't mention the dildos this time."

"How could I have forgotten?" Her cheeks are cold. She doesn't rub at them but lets the salt tears dry, tightening the skin. She turns away from her reflection, comforts herself with some of what's always pleased her in the kitchen to look at—appliances set neatly in a row under the glass-faced cupboards, each atop its own reflection in the gleaming stone of the countertop; built-in range and overhead rack of brass-bottomed pans and Le Creuset fryers; track lighting. She's done all right on her own. She has nothing to complain about, really—nothing to worry over—and yet… "Ben," she says. It's all she can think to say, for the moment. Then, "No. I'm sorry. I deserve every word of that, don't I. Sorry."

"No, *I* deserve you to bite my head off, calling in the middle of the night. What a nightmare conversation!"

True enough, she thinks. "It's OK, honey," she says. Does she rile him up just to comfort herself by providing him this solace afterward? Is this really the only way they can tear down all the defenses? "It'll all be all right." Then, "You wanted those recipes?"

The things we come to believe, she'll think later, remembering this moment, this last little exchange before the recitation of recipes and cooking instructions; she'll be under the trees watching the kids at the park, hell-bent on their eggs and treasures, scavenging under the bushes and leaves: utterly random! Why not believe (in the sense of worship, that is) in the resurrection of worms and beetles as butterflies, say, or of dead bugs in the form of a bat's wings, dead birds in the breath of a cat—something like that, with an actual, tangible physical corollary? Why rabbits at Easter? Why eggs? Why this man on a cross who purposely died for our sins? Why sins? Why, for instance, the saying *a bat out of hell?* Why any of these emblems? Why, of all the possible lives for her and Ben—all the possible types of estrangement, too—these two? Why *did* she go birding that day with Tad? There'd been another man at the time—Ted, his name was—one she'd liked equally well (though she's always forgetting) and who'd phoned her often, and whom she might just as easily have married—well, except for the fact she'd stood him up, accidentally, later that same week of having met Tad, and never heard from him again for years. That, she'd taken as a sign. A sign of her other romantic interests falling away. But always, all of it had been random. Accidental. Sorted and given meaning only in retrospect. (Later, for instance, the man, Ted, had shown up on her doorstep apologizing profusely and saying how horrible it was that *he'd* stood *her* up—he had to explain this and get it off his chest, finally. He was a coward, he said. He'd been called away suddenly for a job and hadn't tried reaching her since then only because of what a heel he thought she must think him.) The instinct underlying belief and order, though, the need for it, this could not be random. It might find its end in some random sign or emblem, but the need was too constant and all-consuming to be accidental. *This*, she'll come to think, *I can believe this.* And she'll want badly then to tell Ben, to say she's OK after all and put his mind at ease. Call him, there on the spot. Fish out her cell phone, push a few buttons and send her voice out into empty space to tell him about it. But no, that would be too intrusive for sure: *Meddlesome mother calling in the middle of younger son's reunion dinner with father and family.* Later, she'll think. Later tonight, when he calls *me*, heartbroken. Drunk and coming apart in the middle of the night because of what the old man said or didn't say, then I'll tell him. I'll mention the trees, too, and how the tops of them appeared to be still in the sunlight while the rest of them were not—as if it were still an earlier time of day up there. The clouds, too, brighter along the tops, pink and shaped like accordions.

BED AGAIN: NIGHT, fan going, awake, alone, and nothing left of the day to enjoy but a slight case of indigestion (too many chocolate covered strawberries and ham with molasses glaze). She's convinced that if ever there was a life to waste, she has most certainly wasted hers. There are facts she could point to in support of this, and she does now. A catalogue of misses, almosts, and failures: the advanced degrees she did not pursue until it was too late to really do anything with them (kids were in diapers and preschool—always too much to do); the research she didn't finish (kids were in school and preschool, and needed her every other waking hour—besides, there were the home-improvements to oversee and endless parenting organizations, all that); the failure of the research she did attempt, finished and unfinished, and the aborted book chapters, articles; the trips she didn't take, money they never had, house they didn't build together (Tad was with that girl, the student, by then; together they had gone off tracking the elusive diphthongs and triphthongs of the great nineteenth-century vowel-shift, through remotest corners of Appalachia and Scotland, while she and the boys—ages six and eight—got by). On and on like that. Dead parents, dead brother, dead cousin, dead college roommate, letter owed to her other college roommate for something like four years now. A list, a ligature in the brain to wake her up, keep her up. It holds her so hard she can hardly think. *I am no one, no one, no one, no one...* Irrational, demented, she knows—considering the many things she has to be thankful for, the many ways she *has* distinguished herself to the people who matter most, the ones she loves; if she could just get herself back into that happier frame of mind.

And then, miraculously, away it all goes. Exhaustion, maybe. Advil finally kicking in. Remembering, perhaps, her last few words with Ben before hanging up—the ones they always say back and forth closing a conversation, no matter how rocky: *Love you, Ma. Well, I never stopped loving you. Never stopped, either.* Often, they don't mention the love part at all, just skip right to the endlessness: *Never stopped. Never stopping either, kid. Not stopping. Me, either...*

She's her other self again now, asleep, drifting back down into the dreams from which she arose. Again, the house is on fire. But this time she's right in it and magically impervious—the heat, flames, smoke, none of it touches her. Her mission here, if she remembers right, is an intriguing one: under the bed is a shoebox full of jewels, some shaped like telephones and accordions, wings and fingers of fluff, others cut more traditionally to resemble the lifelong fidelity of deluded men. Whatever they look like, she must eat them all before running back out to save the woman in the wicker wheelchair— her mother, as it turns out—wheel her back from the cliffside and down the mountain to their getaway. It hurts, but she keeps at it. Sits with her back to the flames and her mouth open. In goes one, in goes the next. Her throat glows painfully—a singer swallowing her song. Pains along her back and shoulders, too, from the flames. Beams crackle overhead, erupt into sparks. Searchlights strobe the smoke and greasy hose-spray. Quick now, time to make a run for it before the man who owns the house and set fire to it hours ago— her husband, the Count of Lapinland, though he doesn't know yet that she knows that she is only the second of his four wives, each on a different continent and unaware of the other (until her recent discovery, that is, of his multiple passports and rabbity style of bookkeeping)—before he can work his dastardly plan, discover her here in the firelight and make his last-ditch attempt to kill her. Faster, faster—no stopping now. She has to get these jewels down, swallow them all, every last one.

No Kind of Music

He sat in one of the lower rows of the balcony section, high enough that the musicians in their black and white appeared to him diminished and foreshortened, but not so distant their sound was lost or tone compromised. He liked to imagine that being this elevated raised his own position within the music, godlike, and that the distance between himself and the players might erase mistakes and mismatched pitches, causing notes to arrive to him sweetened and more perfectly blended, more purely themselves; and he watched the players for evidence of a divine or magical connection to some essential truth within the music moving so uniformly through them, innervating them. He knew this was a fiction—any player up close was a lot of suffering joints and contradictory impulses, bad breath, weak eyesight, creaky digestion (he'd talked with them at fundraiser events and a few times following open rehearsals, enough to have witnessed all of this and more); if there were evidence of magical or divine connections to be beheld in them it showed in the raw skin of their fingertips, bitten nails and torn cuticles, chapped mouths—all the places where they'd worn through themselves trying and trying and loving the music so habitually, so imperfectly over the years. They were only human, after all—mortal, mutable. Nothing in the world was ever otherwise. The search for *essential truths* and *perfection* was probably as delusional as it was invariably empty…he knew this, and yet he also liked to imagine, up there in the balcony seats, watching, feeling a piece as it breathed and came to life, its pulse resuscitated and ticked into being by the conductor's baton after however many hundreds of years in manuscript vaults and libraries, picturing the violins as hearts or lungs, bows vibrating air through them all in unison, he liked to imagine maybe it wasn't empty. Why else did music exist? So his rapture, listening, was composed of equal parts pleasure in anticipating the revelation of a truth he'd never known, longing that he might one day know it, and ecstatic grief at having always been so estranged. Tonight's program—late works of Gyorgy Ligeti and, following intermission, Brahms's Fourth—was no exception, and kept stirring in him emotions he couldn't name... the Ligeti especially, with its cinematic, throbbing impressionism. It could only be followed by something as brooding as Brahms. He wondered if he'd stay for the Brahms after all—if he might not be better off without it. He'd never been much for Brahms, in the best of times.

Over a year ago but not quite two, in the fallout of grief following the deaths of their remaining parents—first his mother, then, within months, his wife's father (her mother having died when she was a child)—his wife had left him for another man. There was nothing new in this. Sick to death of him and the reminders of loss and suffering he must have come to embody for her—all the talk about white blood cell counts, wigs and nebulizers, bed pans, catheters, pneumonia, hospice-care, end of life plans—she'd fled. Taken up with a man four years younger than herself, who had a carbon and titanium contraption for a left leg (to Patrick it looked part gazelle, part Cyborg, with a short springy ski-foot thing at the end of it, more like a small inverted suspension bridge than a foot). He ran marathons and triathlons semi-regularly and was as accustomed to triumphing over all adversities as Patrick and Charlotte had grown accustomed to giving in and expecting the worst. Patrick had recognized this about the man the first time he'd laid eyes on him, at the annual Bloomsday Race, loping crookedly alongside them— creaking, sweating, stride half-flesh half-metal—months before Charlotte had taken up with him. For a while they'd all been friends.

At first, thinking ahead to his new singleness, and later, beginning to settle into it, he'd even felt some excitement about the inevitable change—visions of an eventual, triumphal second life for himself, some woman other than Charlotte beside him—an implicit challenge to survive and better himself, and subsequent surge of darkly-tinged humor about the whole affair to go with it. He'd lost weight, cut his ponytail, got new glasses, capped his teeth and learned to smile more at strangers. But after a time, a few months, less, when the alarm of new loss had expired and he found himself more or less the same as ever but alone and unguarded against a world that seemed slightly modulated from before, unmoored from any personal connections in a way he would never have envisioned for himself, he began his renewed interest in music—specifically, symphonic.

Part of it had to do with his maternal grandfather, who had always wished he'd been a conductor rather than a businessman. Some of Patrick's earliest recollections—from the years in which he and his mother had lived in the grandfather's basement in-law half-suite while she finished her nursing degree and Patrick was often left in the grandfather's care for what seemed like days at a time—involved long afternoons, the two of them alone in his grandfather's study listening through sides of Beethoven, Mozart, Brahms, Bach, Vivaldi, and Sibelius. They'd listen, and if Patrick were able to stay awake through it, if he weren't lulled down by something under the surface of the music—not feeling or rhythm but a logical, picture-generating complexity that was like being in a dream where all thoughts and images somehow derived from an ever-shifting wheel of mathematics—if he kept his attention in the room and didn't drop off, his grandfather would explain. Stern and shamefaced at the same time, but gradually giving in to an affection which overrode his embarrassment at having such hopeless, fruitless aspirations and such a weight of disappointment in himself for never having pursued them, he'd narrate where the musical ideas and themes began and how they built, whistling along tunelessly and waving a finger at the speaker cabinet, pointing at things you couldn't really see; he'd translate how themes replicated themselves and inverted into accompaniment and developed into new themes, new ideas in a relative key, like telling a story or passing from one afterlife into another, or coming up for air after a plunge to the bottom of the lake. So there was something ancestral, almost at the gene-level in his renewed interest in music which on the one hand aligned him (depressingly) with all of his grandfather's failure and abandoned aspirations, and which on the other hand was just plain tranquil. A general giving in and pacification of ambitions which reminded him of those afternoons alone with his grandfather in the study, listening through the crackle of the needle on vinyl, and which he liked to imagine now drew him closer to a true appreciation of whatever he heard. He did not check out books from the library on meter and theory, or score interpretation, did not make half-hearted attempts at decoding the score annotations of the great conductors or shake his head, pencil in hand, tapping with one finger and considering the subtlety of dynamic interpretations. Unlike his grandfather, he could not read a note of music. He did not stand at a mirror, arms upraised, sculpting the air in a mimicry of symphonic sound, stirring his right hand in squares or diamonds or triangles with the beat, cueing invisible horns with his left (all things he'd witnessed his grandfather doing as he sank in and out of his own music-induced sleep). He listened and let his mind drift to the forms he felt articulated inside the music.

His guilty pleasure, if he had one, was reading about the lives of the composers, the better to inform his listening. He liked imagining a world with no cell phones or cars, QuickBooks, Excel, tax codes or keypads. A world defined by the clip-clop of horse-hooves and a grindingly austere metal-ringed carriage wheel rolling over rocks or snow, horse's tail blown back at you in a cold wind; a world where Bach was considered insignificant as compared with the field of then-popular composers, all forgotten now, or where Vivaldi and his two sister-mistresses had disappeared into obscurity, all of his musical legacy abandoned and forgotten until shortly before

Patrick's own birth year. He wasn't anything like systematic about his reading; nothing particular was at stake in it. He skipped around from the classical to the baroque to the romantics and wandered back again, never settling on a favorite period or personality. They'd all been hounds. They'd had their health complications and problems with drink and syphilis and gout and chronic under-employment, and they'd hated each other for any success that wasn't their own, all of them, with the possible exception of Bach.

MEANWHILE, THE DRAMA of life-changing calamities to dwarf his own circumstances had gone on next door without letting up. Marvin and Gina. They'd been permanent fixtures on the block since forever, since long before Patrick and Charlotte had moved in; mid-70's, on their way east from California along I-90 to settle outside Minneapolis, they'd stopped in Spokane and never driven further. *Blew a head gasket,* Marvin told them. *Best damn blown head gasket I ever had, tell you what!* Some of it had to do with money; mostly it was the dry western air, like California but clearer, and the summertime smell of pines—the easy, cheap small town life, then-thriving arts scene, tree-lined avenues, no traffic and the promise of a real winter. They'd parked the van, rented awhile, and when the landlord died, bought the property from his son for a song and never left.

Some Sunday afternoons Patrick used to hear, through screen windows, Marvin inside exclaiming, *Jesus loved my guitar playing this morning!* after which Gina would laugh her smoker's-voice laugh and say something like, *Tell it true! What else did he say?* To which Marvin would reply, *Jeee-eesus loved what I had to say today with the E flat-seven chord! The LORD said to come right home and eee-eeat some PUSSY! The Lord said strip her and take her from behind!* Back and forth like that until, regular as clockwork, the sound of them noisily having sex in the bedroom at the back of their house would follow. For a while Patrick and Charlotte had been half-alarmed, half-amused, hearing this, unsure if their neighbors were jokers or zealots or sex freak exhibitionists or part of some strange sex-and-guitar-playing Jesus cult or all the above. Unsure, as well, whether they were invited to join in or intended not to notice. But over lawn-edging, gardening, mis-delivered mail exchanges, and a dinner or two they came to know more and figured it out. Marvin was a guitarist. He played with several groups around town, anyone with work, really, and one of his regular gigs was at the hugest Life-Culture warehouse ministry on the outskirts of town—a place so big it had its own Starbucks, and Jumbo-tron monitors with closed-captioning for the back of the auditorium and the anteroom overflow crowd. Neither he nor Gina was religious in the least. *Power*, Marvin told him one morning, when he'd come by to borrow Patrick's wheelbarrow. *That church, I tell you what—no lie—that's what it's about, plain and simple. Power. They say give money, the people empty their wallets. They say give more or you're going to hell, and they empty another wallet. They say think this, and the people think it. They say vote like this, the people do. It's surreal, a direct line to that kind of people-power like what we used to talk about in the communist movement or whatever, back in the day. Only it's all so completely fucked up to shit. Anyway, I don't know what you do with it, but it is a rush to be around. Fucking aphrodisiac, I'll tell you what.* Patrick did not let on, when he learned this, that he already knew as much, having heard it through the open windows for some time by then. He'd nodded, laughed. In his own line of work, accounting, he dealt with some charitable organizations, a few churches and one women's shelter, but nothing approaching the size or scale of that church. *It's a multi-corporation is what*, Marvin concluded.

Patrick didn't correct him on this. He said, *I wonder who does their books?*

Jee-eeesus does their books, Marvin said in the same tone of voice Patrick had heard so often through the windows. He went careening around the corner with Patrick's wheelbarrow. *Jee-eeesus does their books and cleans their toilets and hires all the illegal aliens to help. Jee-eeesus says kill the fags...*

A year or two after Patrick and Charlotte had moved in, the

troubles next door began. First Marvin and Gina's daughter returned home with her eighteen-month-old and vanished, leaving the girl, Marcie, behind. Patrick and Charlotte assumed it was an extended visit or some kind of longer-term baby-sitting arrangement while the mother pursued whatever it was, back in Seattle. Only later they learned the mom had dropped the child off in order to save her, and so that she could continue her own escalating drug habit, which had shifted to heroin. The reason they hadn't seen Marvin or Gina around much in the intervening weeks was because they'd been keeping strange hours to nurse the girl through her own withdrawals and to monitor her more or less around the clock.

All of this was relayed to Patrick through Charlotte over a late dinner of cold chicken and couscous, mid tax-season. She was flushed from her after-work swim at the Y; he was exhausted and had the usual crusty, post-work, tax-season feeling that he'd forgotten to drink anything or eat all day—parched and deflated. If he closed his eyes he saw Dali-like grids and columns of his own crisp pencil-written numbers, up and down and across worksheets, marching, marching, none of them adding up. He had the sense, too, as Charlotte told him about Marvin and Gina's situation next door, that decisions about their own childless condition were being edged towards without being spoken outright. This was often the case: they were into the last few years of being viable candidates for in vitro fertilization (Charlotte thirty-six, Patrick forty-two), but were still putting it off, waiting, not deciding. Any mention of children, other peoples' children, pregnancy, grandchildren, even sex, carried the subtext of this unaddressed thing, this tension. On the one hand it was unfair to insist that Charlotte endure the months of hormone treatment leading up to an attempted implantation, not to mention the risk of having twins or triplets, something neither of them wanted but which would unquestionably fall harder on her than on him, if it happened. On the other hand, if she said *Yes, let's do it*, he was sure he'd throw himself right into it alongside her—sure, too, it would please his mother, still alive then, more than just about anything in the world. So, yes, he wanted it. But he couldn't just say so outright. It was a complex tabulation that involved balancing cost, suffering, both of their futures and the moral superiority of her probable preference to adopt. *Why?* she might ask, if he raised the subject now. *Just explain for me. Why do there have to be more Shields babies? What does it matter if there's no one to carry forward the genetic line? There's starving unwanted kids out there. Are you really that vain, Patrick? Is that what this is?*

"What will they do?" he'd asked. He watched her face for signs. Watched her chew and swallow and press a napkin under her chin, though there was nothing he could see to wipe away.

She shrugged. "Give her to us, obviously. Don't you think?" she'd said. "Kidding."

"Funny."

"Free to good home," she said. Smiled mischievously, had another bite and pushed back suddenly from the table. "I want some wine. You? I worked my *ass* off today, *and* I swam a mile. I want to get drunk."

That was an answer, of sorts.

"Still looks pretty good from here," he'd said.

"What's that?"

"Your ass."

"Oh…Patrick. Can't we have one, nice relaxing night together, no pressure, no worries, just *one night*."

"Nothing I can see that's stopping us."

For a time Gina and Charlotte walked together, mornings—most of a fall, sporadically through winter, and less and less as spring came on. Patrick never asked why or what had happened to end it. He assumed it was nothing—the usual attrition of friendship and discipline. Gina's back went out, Charlotte was down with the flu; the routine never found its groove again. But he'd enjoyed it from a distance while it was happening, the ritual and the fact that it seemed to please Charlotte—sweat clothes at her side of the bed and Gina at the door in the early light, sometimes even before dawn, talking too loud; and then crossing paths, Charlotte's hurried, cold-lipped kisses returning as he went out the door to work and she came back in. Once, when she mentioned it, that she missed it, missed Gina, he offered to walk in Gina's place. *We'd have to start a little earlier*, he'd said, *but I'm game.* She'd looked long and earnestly at him until he had to realize she almost didn't know what he was talking about. *We could do that, Patrick. But I don't know. I don't know. Sorry. It's not the exercise I miss so much as the girl-time.*

One rainy evening, early in the season of their own breakup, the friendship must have revived. He witnessed Gina and Charlotte just home from work at the end of the driveway talking, talking and then suddenly they weren't there anymore—they'd gone up the block in the rain still talking and gesturing, mostly Charlotte waving her arms like a conductor, and he'd wondered whose side Gina would take, if that's what was happening. Whose side had she ever been on? Hard to say. He half-entertained the thought of chasing after them with a golf club and swatting them apart, saying, *No, no, you butt out of it already, nosy woman—let her make up her own mind!* But no, he was pretty sure whatever advice or guidance Gina offered wouldn't make much difference for Charlotte, and regardless, steadfast and long-married as she was, Gina would likely come down on the side of staying put. His side. She'd say, *I see the temptation, but honestly…a little more time, huh? Wait for the love to come back around, I always say. You both, you're still grieving.* He'd ask about it later if he saw her.

He never got the chance. Not long after the evening he'd seen them together at the end of the driveway talking, and no more than a month after Charlotte's "official" move out day, while Marvin was downtown at the guitar shop selling guitars and teaching, Gina mis-calculated or mis-combined some of her heart medications, deliberately or not, no one would ever know, and died of a stroke almost instantly. Marcie, the granddaughter, was six or seven years old by that time, probably in afterschool day care when it happened. Patrick was not at home. When he heard the news and tried reaching Charlotte about it he got bumped through to her work and cell phone voicemail so many times he finally decided hell with it, and told her in a message. *This is cold, but you're not answering so I'm just going to tell you straight up and you can deal with it however you like.* Both of them were too overwhelmed with their own troubles to give much attention to anything or anyone else and missed the memorial service. One afternoon, he looked up from whatever he'd been reading, glanced outside, and through the glare of the front window thought for sure he saw Gina coming up the sidewalk in her walking shoes—red hair, freckles, blocky figure and old jeans, too-much makeup; *Jee-eesus told me to eat some pussy*, he heard in his head, as he'd always reflexively heard, like it or not, when he first sighted her—and then realizing it wasn't her, couldn't possibly be her because she was dead, he remembered that the memorial service had happened weeks ago and that he'd completely forgotten and had never even thought to drop by a condolence card or flowers because he'd been too absorbed muddling through his own blown-apart life.

People, he remembered his mother telling him, one of the last few days she lay dying. She'd had to put a finger over the tracheotomy hole at the base of her throat to force air through her voice box and could only speak in short, phlegmy bursts. *They mean well. Mostly. They're not so good. It's never intentional though. You have to. Remember that. Not take it personal. Nobody's. Perfect. They might wish. But they aren't. You included.* A lifetime of work raising him, caring for the sick and elderly, and this was her best parting advice? *Nobody's perfect.* Well, true enough. *Rest, Ma*, he'd told her. *I don't wanna rest. Rest! I want to die already. Sick of it. This. Interminable. What'd that Doc Conklin. Say a week? That's Friday. This is only…Tuesday! How. Much longer? Pat?* Conklin, when he'd estimated a week remaining, had also been somewhat amused at Patrick's mother's impatience to die, and had wondered if there weren't a few old movies she might want to see one last time, favorite music to hear, friends to catch up with. Something, surely. She'd said nothing to any of his suggestions but rolled her eyes at the ceiling and flapped her hands on the bed before looking back imploringly at him. *No*, he'd repeated, he would not help her with anything like a physician-assisted suicide. For a while after, he'd held her hand and finally he'd stood, saying, *This is goodbye then, Mrs. Shields. It's been a pleasure serving as your physician, but... So...* He touched a wrist to his cheek and held out his hand for Patrick. *You call if you need anything.*

More time passed, a year, longer, during which Patrick noticed the yard next door more grown up with weeds and dead grass than flowers. He saw the porch filled with all the junk that once belonged to Gina—an exercise bike, bags of clothing, three sewing machines, bean bag chairs, ancient stereo system, stuff he couldn't even identify—and then the porch cleared away again by one charitable organization or another. Snow came and went. He saw the daughter visiting in various stages of dishevelment, but generally looking more alive and alert than he'd seen her before. What was the tabulation there? Mom dies, daughter begins to rehabilitate? Once, on a whim, he brought by a casserole, and more recently, a pizza and a six-pack. He learned a little about how Marvin was surviving. He'd cut his ponytail as well and had lost some weight. Having retired from gigging and lessons, he planned to spend the rest of his time in the newly empty house raising Marcie and re-mixing and editing archived recordings and footage of live shows from some of the better bands he'd played with in the 70's and the 80's. Maybe he'd get a little solo project going after a while. No more bands, no more church gig. Occasionally, Patrick heard the buzz of an amp snapping on next door, a squeal of feedback and some bent wailing notes, sometimes a few chugging bars of a song, followed inevitably by the sound of a hand released across open strings and the guitar abandoned to a puddle of static hum and reverb beside the amp. One late summer night this went on longer than usual and Patrick had felt hopeful at first, optimistic on Marvin's behalf, tapping his fingers along with the music, trying to catch what it was—sounded like early Credence mixed with some poorly executed Hendrix—but the longer it went on the more he was just annoyed. He banged shut his kitchen window. *Give it a rest,* he wanted to call across the driveway to Marvin. *No music. Please.*

Have mercy. Jesus might have loved it, but I emphatically do not.

Fall tilted again into winter, and one cold night after the leaves had gone but before any snow was on the ground, Charlotte dropped in unannounced for some winter items, still in boxes in the attic—boots, scarves, a pair of mittens knitted for her by Patrick's mother—things she'd evidently done well enough without the previous winter, though it had been a mild one and the winter ahead was predicted to be much worse. Dave, the one-legged runner, was out of town, training or running or both. Patrick didn't necessarily understand or want to understand.

"I'll join up with him next week. Right now he's just cranky. It's R and R week. He's a bundle of nerves and nothing to be done about it."

"R and R?"

"Before the race. You taper and then you stop. Let your body rest."

"Oh, right, sure thing."

"And get to know the course."

"Makes sense."

"But mostly, feet up. Lots of fluid and rest."

He didn't correct her on this. *Foot. Foot up.*

They ended up walking in the new cold, stopping together often to admire the stars, always somehow more noticeable in the cold and against the austerity of bare tree limbs, slick crackle of frozen dead grass underfoot. By the duck pond she faced him abruptly and grabbed his arm but didn't say anything.

"What?" he said. On the other side of the pond some kids were standing together by parked vehicles, laughing, drinking, making too much noise.

"Never mind."

"Never mind what?"

"It's so hard, isn't it. What do you *do* with your days anyway? No, you were always good on your own, weren't you. You don't have anyone new?"

She was standing on his foot and some hair had blown across and gotten stuck on her upper lip which was wet with mucus. Reaching to brush the hair back and at the same time shifting his position so she wasn't standing on his toe, he recognized the liberating absence of any subtext in gestures between them; there was nothing to be implied or misread or over-read in anything he did or said or didn't say to her now. Maybe they'd finally begin to *see* each other again. Maybe they'd come to realize, seeing each other, that they'd never even actually *liked* each other that much to start with. He almost remembered a feeling like that, early on, not long after they'd met and before he'd stopped being able to differentiate between all of his strongest impressions of her—liking, aggravation, sexual attraction, admiration—before those impressions had twisted together into the dynamo of emotions that was a marriage.

"No. No one for me." He shrugged. "Just work. Reading. Go to the symphony sometimes."

"The symphony!"

"What? What's so surprising about that?"

"Just, like…I never would have…" she broke off laughing.

"I like it! What's wrong with the symphony?"

"Nothing *wrong*. I'm laughing…not in a mean way, but because it makes me happy, thinking of you there. Patrick at the symphony! What do you like? Who's your favorite composer?" She tugged him along and the next few steps they walked arm-in-arm.

"I wouldn't say. Anything through the early Romantics actually is fine by me, I guess. After that my interest falls off some…"

Back home again—not theirs anymore, not *his* either, not even *home* so much as a neutral, barren zone wherein he camped out with all of his "stuff"—they sat up late over tea, reminiscing, trading news of friends, killing the time. When he saw her fidgeting to turn her watch around on her wrist, it dawned on him what she must have been trying to say there at the duck pond. She was lonely. More than that, she envied his solitude—some idea about the seeming tranquility of his solitude she must be entertaining, the same way he'd been so aggrievedly envious of one-legged Dave in the beginning.

He supposed this had something to do with the business of being a *whole* or a *half* or *partial* person, an old subject they'd debated off and on in their final weeks and months living together and which he'd never honestly felt he grasped, except to say he understood that she thought he *was* whole while she definitely was *not*. What a *whole* person might be, though, he was never sure—some impossible, philosophical ideal à la Ayn Rand and Deepak Chopra, maybe. Of course, the irony of her having taken up with a man so evidently, physically, *not* whole, and so quickly, didn't bear pointing out.

He reached across the table, covering her hand with his and said, "We're married still. You can stay the night. There's no impropriety."

"Oh, Patrick." She shook her head, but she was beaming and he realized that he'd known, since coming back inside and despite the absence of subtext, that this was probably how the evening would wind up; she, on the other hand, had probably known it from the moment he'd answered her knock at the door.

"It's just us here. No one has to know. Not like it hasn't happened before, right? Where's the harm? I mean, I won't say anything if you won't…"

The whole time, making love to her, he'd known it was their last. Surprisingly, his feeling about that wasn't all sad. Sensations were heightened out of proportion, and perception. He was pretty sure he'd never apprehended another person as fully and clearly, never known as exactly how his own touch registered, and never been as generous with or at ease in his own body responding to her touch; knew, too, even as it was happening, that he would likely never remember a single night of lovemaking as vividly as this one. She kept her socks on through it and fell asleep as she always had, back to him, knees pulled to her chest, sheets drawn tightly around her chin. Once, sliding over top of her, fingers locked through hers and feeling the absence of any metal on her left ring finger, he had an inkling of the abyss ahead—how bad this was going to feel later, tomorrow and the day after—an inkling of what he was losing even as he was in the throes of having it. He kept waking up and drifting back off all night, amazed that the night should last this long, the street light falling through the uncovered window and across his new bed like a ladder of light between them—a bridge or barrier he couldn't say, possibly both. Only after she'd gone and he'd showered and eaten something and sat down again at the table where they'd drank tea the night before, staring into the empty space where she'd sat, the empty day ahead against which he had nothing in store save tonight's program at the symphony—Brahms's Fourth and Gyorgy Ligeti—did it hit him. If she didn't call or write, he might not see or talk to her again until one of them filed for divorce. It would be months or years or never. He would not be the one to make contact. That had never been his role in the marriage and certainly wasn't now, given all that had happened. Now he needed to wait. Until then, he wouldn't see her.

THE LATEST TROUBLE next door had to do with the dog—a pitbull-collie mix with a speckled apron of black and white over its chest, and feet that looked to be two sizes too big for the rest of its frame. Marvin and his granddaughter had inherited it from Marvin's stepson, the older brother of the formerly heroin-addicted daughter, and now didn't know what to do because the dog needed a home. But being part pitbull, it was almost uniformly distrusted or disliked—no one would take it—and there was no question that the girl, Marcie, really couldn't handle much more in the way of personal loss, even a dog. There had to be a limit somewhere. Some months earlier, just after New Years, the uncle, with his dog, had moved up from Portland to help fill the gap and take care of Marcie, and not long after that, late April (tax season wrap-up for Patrick), cycling home for dinner in the rain, the uncle had been run off the road by a drunk driver. Patrick had seen cars coming and going at all hours. He'd heard about the need for long term or permanent dog care because of Marvin's asthma. He'd seen the formerly heroin-addicted daughter, Ann, lurking on the porch, smoking, in exactly the same pose and on the same lawn chair Gina had used. Same red hair, same squarish-figure and small hands. But he hadn't had any updates on the uncle's health until the afternoon he saw Marcie, who had to be eight or nine by now, wandering first one way and then the other, up to the park and back again, iPhone in one hand, leash in the other, gamely trying to figure out how the phone worked, as the dog towed her along.

"New phone?" Patrick asked. He was in his own driveway, done flaming weeds and getting ready to roll the yard-waste bin into the back to make a run at cutting the latest outgrowth of Oregon grapes and then aerating the grass there with the new spike-soled aerating shoes he'd mail-ordered from Lee Valley.

The girl kept her eyes lowered. "It was my uncle's."

"Oh, right. And how—?"

"He's dead. He never came out of his coma." She pulled back on the dog's lead. "*Good dog! Good dog! Behave!*" Lashing its tail side-to-side and gasping, the dog would not be dissuaded from its efforts at pulling her the rest of the way up the driveway to Patrick. "I don't think the phone service is on anymore though, or I can't get to it without the password thing anyway but it looks like he has like forty-eight new messages on his voicemail thing!"

"*Dead?*"

By itself the accident had been too much to absorb. *Impossible. No, no more*, he'd said to Marvin, when he'd first heard the uncle was hospitalized. But he hadn't asked for updates and hadn't heard about the coma because no one had been home there much lately and, honestly, he couldn't fathom more bad news visited on that household. In some way he'd persisted in the false belief that so long as he didn't hear about it, everything might be OK next door. Tax season fully concluded, he'd made his now annual late-spring trip out of town to Banff to hear the symphony and walk by Lake Louise doing absolutely nothing. Returning, he'd figured no news was no more bad news.

"My mom's coming home again, though!"

"Your mom," Patrick had replied, for the moment inexplicably unable to register what she meant.

"Yeah, from Seattle. Week after next? If she gets her own place maybe she'll decide we can keep him!"

She had on a snap shirt he could swear had belonged to Gina, made of faded blue handkerchief material, only there was no way it could have been Gina's, no way it'd fit her, and under that a stretchy white tube top worn in imitation of the mother, he supposed. Huge pink sneakers with glitter-crusted pig-tailed laces engulfed her feet; from these protruded stick-figure legs with backwards bending knees. A kid. How old? Older than her years, anyway. "Keep...who?"

"The dog. Otherwise, Gramp says it's the pound." She sounded almost elated, frenzied, upbeat, winding the hand strap for the dog's leash tighter and tighter around her knuckles; all of this Patrick recognized as the innervation of loss and desperation. Nothing made sense any more in her life. This was the violinist's fingers racing to some point beyond the end of the fingerboard where hearing stopped. It was the silence and the air displaced before the timpanist's mallet struck. It was no kind of music. And then the girl turned and went back up the street, eyes still glued to her uncle's iPhone. He stared after her. *Damn it*, he told himself, *damn it to hell, no*, realizing the thought was in some way directed at Charlotte. *A dog. No. There's no way in hell I can take a dog. Simply no way.*

VIVALDI WAS BEST KNOWN for his flaming red hair and his impossibly virtuosic skill on the violin. Reviewers of the times frequently claimed they'd never heard a violin played as well before and doubted that anyone, ever, would hear it played as well again. He was also an asthmatic and a priest, but gave up the priesthood early, almost immediately after having been ordained, because of the asthma. Most of the middle years of his career he spent employed at Ospedale della Pieta, a girls' orphanage for the bastard offspring of nobility, where he taught stringed instruments and composed concerti, cantatas and sacred music for the girls to play. Later in life, done with the Pieta, he returned to Vienna to compose operas, some of which outraged the public—one, before it was censored, told the story of a woman who falls in love with another woman dressing as a man—all the while living with one of his former pupils, a young singer of some renown, Anna Giro, and her sister Paolina. To anyone who asked, he insisted Anna was his friend and housekeeper, not his mistress. Ditto the sister. Both women were small in stature and unattractive; Anna was said to have a 'fascinating mouth,' many languages at her command, and a huge voice to contrast her small stature. Everywhere Vivaldi went—and he traveled frequently at the end of his career in search of patrons and companies to produce his operas—they went with him: Mantua, Verona, Prague, Berlin. By the time of his death he was destitute and completely disregarded as a composer. His last days he spent convalescing in the home of the widow of a Viennese saddlemaker, suffering from a combination of asthma and bronchitis, slowly dying. His final words, presumably spoken to Anna and/or Paolina, were not recorded. What he'd contributed to western music wasn't known or acknowledged until many, many years later, in the mid-1950's, when some scores were re-discovered by a French music historian. All those years they'd lain moldering in vaults at the Pieta and in the desks and trunks and armoires of great-great-great nieces, nephews and many-times removed cousins throughout Italy. From the recovered work there began to emerge a revised picture of Vivaldi's significance and his influence on subsequent composers—specifically his innovations with the concerto and opera forms and ways in which he'd built upon and improved Corelli's use of sequential harmonic patterns, later taken up by Bach—and before long, a revival of all of his work and a newfound passion for his highly engaging, necessary and playable melodies. How had the music world ever gotten by without him?

Patrick's own hair had started falling out sometime in his mid-twenties and had never had any real eye-catching luster or attributes anyway, let alone being red. He did not suffer from asthma and had no interest in Catholicism. He'd never known any nobility or been to an orphanage of any kind and couldn't read a note of music. One of his roommates in college had been a violinist and had tried, three times, to teach Patrick to hold it and to play *Twinkle, Twinkle*—that was the full extent of his experience with the violin. The more technical the analysis and discussion of Vivaldi's influence on western music grew, the more numbly he felt his brain responding to the information until all he wanted was to close the book and hear some of what they were picking apart—pivot chords and appoggiaturas and sharp seven chords, sequential patterns... More important for him, in the background of Vivaldi's sweetly resonant string figures was the imagined personal history of the man—the pictures he saw generated in the music: one, a black, covered carriage topped with trunks, a woman's slip or crinoline caught under one of the door frames, weak dust clouds eddying behind it and from beneath the horses' hooves, pulling up to the opera house in Vienna or Mantua, the door swinging open and Vivaldi emerging, one calf and buckle-topped shoe, then the other...then Anna. Then Paolina. Another, an orchestra of young girls in white orphanage frocks, pomegranate flowers in their hair, playing, Anna Giro with her small hands and fascinating mouth probably among them, all half in love with each other or with Vivaldi himself, or both, all parentless, disenfranchised, barred from ever having a life of any meaning in the world, but having instead the privilege of this existence comprised of nothing but singing and playing the music of Antonio Vivaldi all day, every day. How bad could it have been? Horribly, wonderfully bad. Sometimes, listening and envisioning this, reading along about the theoretical nonsense that meant no more to him now than it had when he was a child, hearing his grandfather interpret, Patrick felt on the verge of grasping the essential missing piece, the perfect, platonic, missing *thing* in his appreciation of music, and simultaneously convinced that whatever it was, whatever was missing, didn't exist or else was impossible to be known by him. But what if Vivaldi had never been re-discovered? What other un-re-discovered music of influence might be out there, unheard? Was the world full of better, unheard music? Did it matter? Now Vivaldi's melodies were downloadable as ringtones and you were hard pressed to find a restaurant where one of his Four Seasons wasn't in constant, heavy rotation as part of a background soundtrack meant to inspire diners to feel hungry and privileged, part of some imagined luxury caste of baroque-music-loving elite. A complex, contradictory, suffering, celebrated, neglected, melody-making virtuoso in life; a cliché after death. What did you do with this information? Only if you listened closely, inside the music maybe somewhere, something was revealed…maybe just the picture of the girls of the Pieta with their pomegranate flowers… all those notes Vivaldi must have composed and arranged specifically, lovingly or not, to be played by *those* fingers, all taught by him, all with problems and idiosyncrasies, strengths and weaknesses he must have known intimately—every note for those specific fingers, that specific skin. There had to be something in it, some leftover physical energy in the connection. He listened. He felt it. He swung his head in time with the music. He got up to turn the music off because the doorbell was ringing through and above it.

Charlotte, he thought, even before he'd touched the doorknob or turned the key in the lock. Had to be. Who else would drop in on a Saturday afternoon? But why, and what would she want now? He'd have to tell her about the dog and the uncle. It had been a week or two already since he'd found out about it. Maybe she and Dave or one of their more athletic crowd would be interested in adopting. Good for a little wrenchingly poignant reminder of old times, he supposed, though what he might hope to gain from that, he couldn't say for sure. *Remember Gina and Marv? The kid next door? Right. Yeah…well, you won't believe it… No, I'm not kidding. Puts things in perspective, doesn't it though? Run off the road by a drunk driver. Twenty-one days in a coma, boom. Like it's biblical payback or something. Divine retribution for all that crazy talk about Jesus and eating pussy!*

They'd spoken only once since the night she'd stayed, a few weeks later when she called to ask if he'd happened to see a gold hoop earring anywhere, by the bed maybe, or in the bathroom. *Kind of bell shaped, with a couple of diamond flecks. Check again*, she said, when he reported that no, there was no such earring in the house. Then, *Oh whatever. I'll make something up. Lost it at the Y or whatever. He won't care that much. It'll be fine.* From here the conversation had meandered on until he realized the lost earring wasn't what she'd been calling for in the first place. She was having doubts and wanting something assuaged or settled, wanting some kind of encouragement or confidence booster maybe, though it hardly bore pointing out he was no longer the one in a position to offer confidence or encouragement for her actions. *You don't miss me at all, do you,* she'd said. Then, *Can't say I blame you.* And after he'd assured her this wasn't true and that of course he missed her, she'd said, *What, though? What do you miss about me, Patrick? Name one thing.* This, he hadn't known how to answer. In his experience there weren't words for those kinds of things. Hair, eyes, nose, skin, voice, laugh, smell—air displaced by her movement across the room, a certain richness of feeling he'd had entering a room she was in already, seeing her there... How did you choose? How did you talk about any of that?

You, he'd answered finally. *I miss you.*

Evidently it was not the answer she was after.

You think about it, and when you have it figured out, I don't know, maybe that's the key. Maybe then we could talk again, she'd said. He hadn't asked her, *What? Talk about what?* He'd grunted an agreement and let it go. What *she'd* realized, she said, running right on, what she missed most about *him* after all this time (so apparently it was something she'd been thinking about; possibly why she'd made the call) was the thing that had also always somewhat riled her: that he didn't live in a million moments simultaneously in his head. He was not like the rest of the world in this one way. *Two, maybe three places at the most. That's it. But it's like you always used to say...your whole thing. All you wanted was the chance to sit alone in the quiet, meditating on your tax codes and amortization schedules and earnings tabulations until everything's worked out. Right? That's you. In a nutshell, that's you. Everyone else, we're Tweeting and texting and calling each other while we're driving, and thinking about shopping lists and car repairs and new clothes and so-and-so's crush at work, all at the same time we're trying to close the sale on that house by remembering the husband's favorite baseball team and where the wife went to high school, kids ages and what's the weather for Thursday anyway, which properties show best in rain or snow, and what are interest rates doing this week? And, oh, what's Dave going to want for supper if it's day twenty-three before the race? It's nuts.*

Busy, he said. *You've got a busy brain. I always said.*

But do you like it, Patrick? Is that what you miss? It was kind of a serious compatibility issue though, wasn't it.

He hadn't answered at first. Then after a pause, though he knew, even as he began saying it, that his words would not reach her in any meaningful way or convey half of what he intended (even he heard how much it resembled one of his mother's aphoristic nuggets), *Well, sure. But isn't compatibility just the way you agree to disagree about things? I mean, what two people don't have incompatibilities...*

This hadn't been the answer she was looking for either, and soon after she had to go.

Ciao, she said. *Call when you can. Call.*

He'd never called.

On the porch was a package for him—more books. No Charlotte.

He watched after the FedEx delivery man, first disappointed, then relieved. Saw him swing up the steps of his truck, wave, crank the engine and rattle up the block, side door still open wide. The light stung his eyes, too bright, too liquid, and he felt a catch in his throat—possibly a carry-forward from the music and the state he'd worked himself into, listening, reading, thinking about that last conversation with Charlotte; possibly a recognition that this was one of those perfect afternoons you wait for a lifetime or a year to behold—clear, warm, dry, smells of flowers and pine trees on the breeze, sun past its apex, still high enough to burn, but mellowing westward into evening. Perfect, really. Spotless. And expiring. And as suddenly as the feeling welled in him it drained away. Because like a picture from that other era of his life, there was Gina on the porch across the drive in a tank top and frayed jeans shorts, smoking, waving a hand at him and calling to him, saying his name. "Patrick? Mr. Shields?"

He nodded, waved back, and as if that were the signal she'd been awaiting, she stubbed out her cigarette on the railing, pocketed it, stood, and came mincingly, barefoot down the steps toward him and across the driveway. Same blocky hips and tough, muscled legs, faint pink patch above one knee from how she'd been sitting, legs crossed, elbow propped on a thigh. A smell of baby powder and cigarettes, something minty with it, preceded her. "Mr. Shields?" Gina absolutely, but twenty years younger. And now as she came closer he registered all the differences, too—darker hair at the roots, darker eyelashes, more gracefully arched eyebrows, thinner through the neck and shoulders. Thinner, period. The eyes, more violet than ice, offset by the darker eyelashes, were hard to look away from and had an undertow of wickedness or fun-seeking devilry that seemed to recede and vanish into sadness the instant you perceived it. She stopped directly below him. "I just thought I'd say hi. Haven't seen you in an age. Ann."

"Right! Ann. Hi. I was just talking to…the other day, Marcie said you'd be home. So sorry about…"

"How's Charlotte?"

They'd spoken at the same time.

He blinked. Leaned closer and came out from inside the doorway a few steps onto the porch. "She's gone. We split. Didn't your dad tell you?"

"Not my dad."

"Marvin?"

"Stepdad."

This didn't make sense. They were both stepkids then? Marvin had adopted and was now raising a grandkid who was not even his own? "Oh," he said. "Anyway, we were both…I was just so sorry to hear about your brother's passing. I can hardly imagine, especially so soon after…you know. Your mother. I had no idea 'til just the other day."

She sighed. "I'm not going to lie, Mr. Shields. It's been tough."

"Please. Patrick. Call me Patrick."

"OK then, Patrick. I won't lie. It's been really, very tough."

"Anything at all I can do to help. You know. You all should ask. It's just me here now."

"Well…" Here she turned slightly and faced back down the street, arm raised to shield her eyes from the sun a moment and affording him a view through the arm hole of her tank top he couldn't help but think was somewhat calculated. How old was she? Late twenties? Older. Not much. Under the shoulder strap of the tank and bisected by a pale blue bra strap was a small rose tattoo, cartoonishly pretty. The sunlight through the front of her tank top turned the skin inside some kind of impossible, tropical apricot color. Again she faced him. "Since you ask. Want a dog?"

"*Within reason,* anything at all." He laughed and shook his head. "No dogs. No livestock, inclusive of dogs. I'm not," he flapped his arms awkwardly, "sadly, an animal person. A fish, maybe, or a snake, though likely as not I'd kill that as well."

Terrible joke, though she didn't seem to mind or to notice. Her laugh was almost identical to her mother's but shaded differently. He couldn't put a finger on it, but where Gina's laugh had somewhat rattled him, tending to make him feel as if he'd been left out of the joke, Ann's did not. Ann's drew him in like the inner workings of music, wanting to be nearer, better understood.

"Well then, Patrick, how's about a drink."

"Sure. I don't actually…don't know what I have in the house. But you're…"

"Oh, I'm of age!" The laugh modulated jarringly to a giggle and that fast, Patrick saw what this had been about all along, what was next—what she hoped to use him for. Just a drink. "Don't worry your head about that!"

"Well," he said, and stooping to pick up his packet of books, stood back for her, holding the door. "Like I say, I don't know what I've got on hand, but I'm sure there's something." One drink. It couldn't hurt anything. Then he'd send her back across the driveway, home. Tonight was the season-opener evening outdoor concert in the park so there was that limit in sight. Maybe he'd walk back over with her and invite them all to come, Marvin, Ann, and little Marcie—hear a little Berlioz and Brahms under the stars, the final two movements of Vivaldi's Seasons. They could lie out on a blanket together listening, drink some wine and watch for shooting stars. Music in an outdoor setting never really did much for him, always seemed somehow ancillary or too backgrounded. Too faint and conspicuously out of its element. But that could be all right, he supposed, in good company. More of a social thing. "Let's see what I can find…"

There were points at which he could have stopped her and later he would wonder about these, why he didn't—what weird combination of propriety, embarrassment or just stupid passivity kept him from acting. First there was the blindedness of coming back in out of the sun—disorienting, transitional—and some way that shift accentuated the out-of-placeness of her presence in his house and their total lack of any common ground, anything to say to each other, putting him off his guard. He could have stopped her before she'd located the bottle of scotch and said childishly, *Mr. Balvenie! There you are! We've been looking for you all over! Bad, bad Mr. Balvenie bo-weenie!*—a fourteen-year-old, expensive, aged in sherry casks, liter-sized bottle because he'd bought it from the duty-free on his way back from Banff—and carried it by the neck to the couch. He could have insisted on pouring for them both, maybe gotten smaller glasses from the hutch in the kitchen and instructed her on the finer points of savoring a single-malt, slowly; could have done more than stare and say, *Uh…whoa there, that's kind of expensive stuff, are you…?* when she filled her glass with what had to be ten-twelve ounces of it and drank about half of it off in seconds flat. He could have taken the glass from her before she'd drained most of the rest of it. Any time after that he could have lifted her by the wrists from the couch and propelled her across the room and back outside, said, *Go, now, and don't come back*. Later, he pictured himself doing this and any number of things to block her, slow her down, and knew it would have been right for him to do so. But he didn't. Didn't do anything. She was a train barreling off the tracks in ways that seemed to him as familiar as they were predestined or inevitable. Clearly this had happened to her before and would happen again, over and over, as long as she lived. He watched her collapse there on the leather couch cushions against which she looked almost superimposed in her torn shorts and tank top, and then he watched her bounce up and teeter crookedly down the hall for the bathroom with the still mostly full Balvenie bottle in hand. He listened to the water dripping into a cup in the sink, saying, *point? point? point?* over and over, and he wondered why he'd never been the kind of person for whom meaning was given in action, why action of any kind had never mattered for him in a defining way half as much as some other essential hidden thing *inside* the action—some kind of meditative secret logic, the perception of which mostly held him up, kept him sidelined, secluded, watching, judging, saying nothing. Maybe it was because of what Charlotte had said about him—that he didn't think ahead, didn't get ahead of the moment or outside it? Actually he didn't think so. It was something deeper-seated, unrelated—some kink in his soul, the source of which was God knows where. And that was the thing about Charlotte—possibly the thing he'd loved best about her and now missed: that she was always pointing out these aspects of his nature, drawing conclusions and half the time steering him wrong, but still showing him things he hadn't known in the process. For *her* it was always action, action, action, figure out your intentions later, if at all. For most people, he supposed, it was like that. So, then…what was wrong with him? Now there was a drunk, strange woman whose life had been recently destroyed by tragedies of every order, and who had a history of drug and alcohol abuse, in his bathroom with a bottle of scotch, possibly on the brink of alcohol poisoning. *Love thy neighbor*. Yes…but *how much*, and at what expense, and anyway *how* exactly were you supposed to love the neighbor who was drinking herself to death in your bathroom on your scotch because of the terrible things that had happened to her over which you had no control? He watched the curtains spin inward with the breeze that carried the same lavender, pine-tree, hot tarmac and barbecue smells that had convinced him, lullingly, moments ago, that he was on the verge of something wonderful and/or that this was one of those perfect days you wait for and need to somehow hang onto, keep forever from passing. What had changed? Everything and nothing.

He stood and started down the hall.

"Hey, Ann." He tapped on the door. No response. "Ann?" He turned the doorknob. Locked. Of course. "Hey, Ann! Are you all right in there?" He banged a fist on the door. "Can you give me an answer here?" Kicked the lower panel of it softly and knocked some more. Remembered that there had been some question as to whether or not Gina had knowingly mis-combined heart medications in order to off herself, and wondered if this wasn't something genetic he was now up against and if he wasn't about to deliver a third dead family member to that poor little kid. Wondered about disassembling the lock mechanism, where his screwdrivers and other tools were, a hacksaw even, sledge hammer, how much time he might have and whether or not he should go across the driveway and enlist Marvin's help. "HEY!" he yelled again and this time heard something like wretching inside, a faint cough and plop-plop sound, maybe the hiss of a zipper. "Hey! Look if you're OK, just say. Otherwise, open…"

The door swung open fast and at first, in the uneven half-light of the hallway, he could not at all be sure what was happening. Arms around his shoulders, too close for him to see anything or to fully register the fact that she was completely naked, she fell against him—a heavy, pliable and mostly anesthetized slickness against which he needed to support himself, at the same time as supporting her. There was nothing to grab onto and no way to steer or direct her. "Hey, whoa, whoa, whoa, what—Ann, what the heck…" He danced with her across the hall to his bedroom and spun her through the door, step, step, step, realizing as he conducted her the last few yards, that though she seemed barely able to stand, her arms had a vicious strength from hell, still locked around his neck and shoulders, and that he could do nothing to break her grip on him. Which was fine, for now, probably a good thing even, because he needed her to hang on or he would not be able to help her. "Steady, steady," he said and spun her again, lowering her onto the bed. Still she wouldn't release him and for a few weird minutes he found himself collapsed on top of her, one leg between hers, more or less reflexively kissing her back, if only to get her to release her hold on him, pushing into her and back away from her, both at the same time.

"Whassa matter Msster Shields? Don't wanna party? Les'sparty! Kissy kissy? Come on. Les'sparty!"

"Shh, shh," he said. Allowed her mouth to open around his, numbly sucking, tongue swirling around his, breath blowing hot and cold across his face.

She jerked her head away. Said, "'Asts disgusting." Made faint spitting sounds.

He stroked his hands along her waist. "OK," he said. "It's OK now. Just relax. Easy, easy."

"Juss thought we could party."

And as suddenly as she'd latched onto him she went completely slack.

He stood back from her.

"Ann?"

The eyes stayed closed, mouth open, one arm straight out, the other at her side. One leg out straight on the bed, the other bent and cantilevered over the edge of the bed. So. He bent, lifted the leg onto the bed and lifted both feet as far to the right as he could. At the opposite side of the bed he tugged the bedspread toward himself until she was more fully in the bed's center and less at risk of rolling herself out of it, then folded the excess bedspread cloth from his side over top to cover her. Turned her head to the side and went into the bathroom for her clothes, which he set by the bedside, and returned again for the scotch. A few inches remained at the bottom of the bottle. A third of a glass on the coffee table by the couch still, two-three fingers in his own glass. The rest of the bottle was now inside her and working its slow way through her cells and pores and liver, expiring a little with each heartbeat and exhalation. She might have gone to the edge, might in fact *live* on the edge more or less full time, but this time anyway, she hadn't killed herself.

He sat down beside her on the bed. There were things he'd like to say to her now—to anyone who would listen, actually—beginning with the story of him and Charlotte, how they'd waited and waited to start a family and finally, when it was almost too late, had consulted specialists to learn that the problem was a simple one having to do with mis-matched PHs and some way natural implantation was just always going to be difficult for them. Not impossible. Difficult. Highly unlikely. A natural, biological incompatibility to throw in with the other psychological, sexual incompatibilities so engrained in the marriage he hardly noticed them anymore. So they waited some more and did nothing, got older, knowing it was solvable, fixable—there was a way forward—and knowing, too, it was a gamble. Waiting was a gamble. Going through with in vitro was a gamble, a more expensive gamble and potential health risk. Pretending nothing was wrong was a gamble of a different kind. And in the end...nothing. "There is such a thing," he wanted to say to Ann, "as waiting too long. You have a daughter..."

But there was no sense talking to a near-dead, passed-out stranger.

He got a mixing bowl from the kitchen and set it by the bedside as well, in case. Turned her head that way again because she'd moved in the interim, and stroking the hair from her forehead, was relieved when she pushed back reflexively against his hand, lips moving to shape words he couldn't hear.

THAT NIGHT HE DID NOT HEAR anything in the music and he was not enraptured. Part of it was his position, at the back of the crowd, acres of people in lawn chairs and on blankets between him and the orchestra, the orchestra on a raised, black, multi-tiered dais under floodlights, some kind of clamshell sound-reinforcing baffle structure suspended behind and above them on wires and scaffolding. The sound wasn't bad, but it wasn't right either—thinned and piped in, canned almost, as if brought from another reality. And they definitely weren't playing their best. The conductor trotted out and back again for curtain calls, despite the absence of actual curtains, and spoke in his European accent about the music on the evening's program; he raised his arms the same as ever and lunged into it, dancing, flinging his arms in an approximation of the sound that welled around him, no backbone beat to be discerned in any of his antics, all of it a fraction of a second delayed from the music reaching Patrick at the back of the park so it made him almost queasy to behold. Up closer he supposed, the focus would be as intense as ever, the usual classical music listening protocols adhered to. Here on the outskirts were people talking and laughing quietly, chatting into phones and snapping pictures of each other. Kids with iPods, one earbud in, one out, roamed, hands aglow with private messages texted to the ether and back again at each other. *Sup? Im here. Where R U? R U K?* And somewhere in that small sea of people was Charlotte with titanium-legged Dave and their new friends whose names he'd already begun to forget. Earlier, almost as soon as he'd arrived at the park she'd found him and grabbed his arm. "Patrick!" she'd said. "I thought I'd see you here! Come! Come join us. How wonderful! We're having some bubbly." So he'd hopped after her through the islands of couples and families on blankets with dinner baskets and cold drinks in Styrofoam cup holders, plastic glasses of wine. Sat a moment and said hello's around to Dave and the other couples with them, and then feeling sadder than sad, realizing he didn't belong here, Charlotte or no-Charlotte, had stood and wound his way back out to the periphery again on one excuse or another. "I like it better further back," he said. "Need to meet some people I think. No, no, it's OK. Sound's better back there. Anyway, gotta use the gents."

So, that was a part of it. A big part of it. Seeing her and knowing he did not in any way belong with her or beside her, if he ever had. The other part was the drunken half-annihilated woman at home in his bed and some way he couldn't shake the picture of her, rolled in under his bedspread, skin slick with alcohol sweat. He'd thought, when he first saw Charlotte, maybe he'd tell her all about it, maybe her and Dave together; but when he'd gotten to them on their blanket, with the other people crowded around on every side, and started thinking about words he'd use to string it together for them, thinking as well that he needed to ask if any of them might be interested in dog adoption, he saw just how it would play in their heads—the obvious lewdness and despair—and knew he couldn't go through with telling it.

Why, though? he wondered. Why wasn't he part of anything, anywhere, ever? Not part of Charlotte or her group or any of the crowd gathered to hear music he ostensibly cared about and had spent half the afternoon reading about; not part of the music either, being neither musician nor scholar nor historian, and having nothing whatsoever in common with Antonio Vivaldi, except for the music that he loved because it put him in mind of his dead grandfather and of orphan girls and maybe hundreds of other things. Sickening to think the closest connection he had in the world just then was to that drunk woman tacoed under his bedspread at home. Before leaving he'd checked on her, and again smoothing the hair from her forehead, had been pleased and relieved at the way she pushed back against his hand, receiving comfort. It wasn't nothing. It was, quite possibly, *less* than nothing.

He turned and started walking away from the sound, up and into the dark outskirts of the park—walking, walking until the music had all but faded to inaudibility and there was only the sound of his own footfalls, his breaths in and out. Wind in the trees. An airplane humming by. Soon the sky would light up, etched with fireworks.

Part of the annual outdoor series-opening concert shebang—a climax of gunpowder crackling open the sky mostly in time with the music, bursts of color and matched timpani together saying the same old tired, exuberant things about being alive. Nothing he wanted to hear just now. If he went fast enough maybe he'd get to some point far enough out he wouldn't have to. There would be nothing then but the music in his own head and the stars from which it had come.

LUCK

HERB ZACKOWSKY WAS NOT A BETTING MAN. His father, small, with a swirl of black and white hair and paunchy, bulldog cheeks, had spent his days at the horse track. Many days, not all of them. Growing up, Herb knew about this indirectly, from the smell on him, booze and track dust and hard luck sweat, and from the cryptic numbered track receipts that lined his jacket pockets and drifted to the back of the front hall closet and sometimes showed up in the laundry, rolled and hard as pills. His father had a weak, creaking voice and watery eyes but his grip was cutting, and he seemed frequently at the end of his patience. When he was angry a shiny patch of sweat or misted spittle would show on his chin and lower lip, gleaming and slightly reddened as if the skin there had been scraped or polished, and his eyes turned opaquely lusterless. Times he came home from the track with a wad of cash were not necessarily guaranteed much better than times he came home without: he'd be more spritely, winnings in hand, talkative, and quick on his feet—more likely to slap and poke you lightly, meaning no harm, but still not smiling much and no less likely to break, suddenly and without warning, stare blankly and come after you with his belt in a fist. *Nervous little fucking Polack Napoleon,* he and his brother would call him. And later, *Capricious dickhead.* Later still, *Who was he—did you ever feel like you knew the guy? Did anyone?*

Herb's brother, Ned, had had his troubles, too, though to Herb's knowledge all that was water under the bridge. They hadn't been close at the time, Herb and Ned—hadn't been close ever, really, not for years, since Ned moved away—but he understood, from the letters and phone calls, the occasional heart-to-heart at family gatherings, that for a time it'd been rough. Really rough. Ned had lost a house and a boat and several rental properties. A backhoe. His marriage had been ruined. Now happily remarried, he and his new wife belonged to one of those extreme Life-Culture Christian churches and this obsession seemed to have as neatly and fully supplanted the whole gambling trouble as imaginable—had set him right on the straight and narrow. And though Herb was glad to think of his brother as finally having escaped that particular money-devouring, money-stricken hell, he was not convinced the problem was really *fixed*. In his mind, the two things were connected, the church and the gambling: Ned was still playing the odds. The stakes had changed, the terms of the game, but he was still placing his faith in a magic conversion—betting one thing against the other, and hoping to be so much better off in another life.

Never Herb, though. He'd tried a few times, but the gene for it must have skipped him, the luck, or the head. *No pleasure in risk*, his life-motto might have been. He just didn't see the point. Didn't get the thrill, winnowing the odds, forecasting and multiplying your winnings, spitting three times for good luck, touching your forehead, crossing yourself, squeezing your lucky rabbit's foot, whatever charm you thought would give you the magic edge against the bookie or the dealer: sweet easy success and the wad of free green in hand. He loved money, but preferred it straight up, earned and not won.

Margo, Herb's wife, had not bet either—that he knew of. Thirty-three years married and there she was now, in the ship's casino, and sitting her fourth straight day at the same bank of one- and five-dollar slot machines, a plastic dish of fake coins like a doggie bowl in her lap and that stupid, rapt look on her face—the one that made him reflect, involuntarily, on his father and mostly estranged brother.

He'd been by twice that morning, so far—first, on his way to the Neptune Lounge for a lecture on totemic art, and later, bored with the lecture, heading back to the main service desk to speak with the woman there about signing on for one of the guided port-of-call excursions, for tomorrow. No walking this time, he insisted. Their first excursion, which had involved viewing of glaciers and wildlife, on-foot, had taught him better: the spinning sea-sickness of his first two days on board had returned in reverse, setting him at odds with every steady surface, so he felt intolerably drowsy, head-achey and squeezed inside as if his guts were on a slow spin cycle. He had no desire to repeat the experience.

"There's the fishing excursion, which is actually quite nice, or the glacier trip again, eagle watching, helicopter tour, or…" Here the woman drew a breath. "Actually, that's what we've got in Juneau, Mr. Zackinski. And of course there's always…"

"Zackowski."

"There's always *shopping* downtown." She smiled and squinted a moment as if some distant, pleasing thought had captured her attention.

"I don't want to go shopping."

"Well, you can stay on the ship, too, if you like. Hardly sucks, if you ask me. It's entirely up to you. The El Dorado lounge is open 24-7."

Where did they get off talking like that? *Hardly sucks.* As if he were her foul-mouthed cussing old uncle or something. *Hardly sucks what?* he pictured himself saying. He grunted and poked at the glossy three-fold flier on the table between them. Depicted on its front fold was a bunch of joy-stricken tourists on a small boat, strangled in orange life-preservers and leaning over a railing to mug for the camera.

"Don't wait too long though. I've only got a few seats left on the Lucky Lady."

"So it's a book-now-or-never type situation, you're saying?"

Again the girl squinted. He'd been wrong about her. Thought

she'd be perky and accommodating. Friendly. Willing to explain things for him in a way that wasn't so condescending, maybe even cut him a special deal. It was because of the copper eyes and the smile, he realized—the mild, benificient smile that pulled her swollen upper lip back from her front teeth and put him in mind of his older daughter, the dead one, Desiree. But this was just a put-on. To her he was more fodder: another befuddled tourist. Sure enough, with his floppy sun hat, digital camera around the neck, and the draw-string pants with the mesh bits and extra zippered pockets, all supposedly contrived to make you appear relaxed and ostentatiously holiday-spirited (though in truth they just made you seem a grown fool in diapers), he looked the part. Just another cranky old rich guy waiting to have his multiple pockets picked clean.

"Well, I'll run it by—"here he paused, considering his options—*the bag, the old lady, the boss, my better half*—"run it by my pretty young wife." She was younger, after all, by a few years, if not especially pretty anymore.

"You do that Mr. Zank…Mr. Zankowski and get right back to me."

Later, with Janelle, on their way for more ice cream from the endless ice cream sundae bar, he passed the casino a third time. Again, the smell of cigarettes coming from its arched doorways; again, the flashing lights and beeping, electronic-chiming machine noises and the piddly clink of fake coins cascading through a chute, someone crying out with pleasure. There she was still, up on her stool, right where he'd last seen her.

"You worry too much, Dad," Janelle said. "Come on. It's harmless fun."

He squeezed her arm in his more tightly. What were the odds, he wondered (speaking of odds)—him with his snaggle teeth and bow-legs, Margo with her slumpy shoulders and sucker-punched look of eternal astonishment—what were the odds of their having created such a winsome, model-pretty beauty? What were the odds, for that matter, of their first daughter being run off the road by a drunken driver?

"Once she loses ten grand—then you'll let me worry?"

"Give her a break."

"Give *her* a break! She dumped seventeen hundred bucks into that thing already—and that was as of last night! Seventeen hundred bucks, gone," he snapped his fingers, "nothing to show for it." Here he tripped against a fold in the carpet and, stumbling, felt the almost pleasurable (because newly familiar) dilation of his senses to accommodate the ship's movement—his inner ear's workings attuned to this new, more fluid, apprehension of balance, space and line.

"Dad. She's not Uncle Neddy."

"I know who she is, kiddo!"

But he didn't—not since getting on this ship, anyway—and that was the problem. She'd drifted straight into the pack of gaming, bingo-playing old ladies. Had become almost instantly indistinguishable to him from the rest of them with their dyed hair and warty necks and necklaces as outlandishly oversized as the opinions they flaunted at the slightest provocation. Just the previous night he'd caught her going on, in a phoney accent, to one of their table mates about overcooked ceviche. "Ceviche," he'd broken in (he knew about this—had had it a few times, in southern Spain no less), "is a raw cuttlefish. Isn't even cooked, they just set it overnight in some citrus juice till it goes tender. From the acid. *You've* never had it, that I know of." Here she'd angled at him the kind of imperious rich-lady glare he was almost coming to expect of her. *Quit putting on airs*, he'd wanted to say. *You're a farmer's kid from Yakima, and you always will be.* "That's not what we're talking about," she'd said. "If we want your advice about washing machines, we'll ask, Herb. Otherwise…" And then the hour upon hour squatting at those damn machines, pumping his money into oblivion. What was that about, anyway? If the ship had stolen his center of gravity and confidence, causing him to think of himself as more or less anonymous, it'd had the reverse effect on his wife—and perhaps in an exact apportionment, who could say?—empowering her and giving her this astonishing belief in herself, her judgment and entitlement.

Worse, in spite of it (because of it?), he couldn't stop himself bragging and putting on airs at every opportunity. Later in the same dinner conversation that had touched briefly on overcooked ceviche, he'd heard himself rambling on. "Started with the TV ad we had back in the early nineties—you're from Seattle, you've probably seen it. The little guy in the tights and joker hat, running around the showroom floor sticking SOLD signs on washers and driers and what have you? *No one beats crazy Zack's crazy prices*! Wasn't me, as you probably deduced. Some of the sales staff though, they started calling me *Zack*, on account of it, which apparently seemed to stick—so the new stores, too, some of them, we dropped the *owski* part. They're just Zack's. Zack's Home of Appliances. Spokane, I think, and Walla Walla and the ones in La Grande and Portland. Those ones are all Zack's." This was a point that had burned him, initially: the way the advertising firm had so delicately insisted on the employment of that foolish little actor look-alike to star in the ad which should rightly have featured him—should rightly have constituted his fifteen minutes of fame, and more. *Think of him like a stunt double,* they'd said; and, *You wouldn't want to do this, would you?* Well, yes, actually, he would. And then the irony of it. Some other guy's antics causing *him* to be re-named, rich overnight, and so many of his franchises called by another name. He was a little proud of himself, now, mentioning it so offhand, as if it were nothing. Then, catching himself in the pride, embarrassed by it, and embarrassed for the whole stupid business, the charade and the vanity. "That guy, though, the actor—Melvin something, wasn't it honey?—he was definitely my likeness. Chose him for it. And I didn't see the *point* in that really—coulda done it myself, without the hat and the tights and whatnot of course, but let me tell you, it was one successful campaign. Went all over the Northwest with it. Crazy Zack!" He popped his hands together, leaned over the table, put on his best imitation of the actor's voice. "'See Crazy Zack for lucky deals at Zackowski's

Home of Appliances!' My secret, see—always make sure your fixed overhead and inventory costs pace your net gains and revenues at a 3-1 ratio. Eh? See where I'm going with that? Always a step ahead of the game." Must have been the wine and the bloody marys making him say so much.

Now Janelle was tugging him up the swaying carpeted stairwell to the promenade deck, having said something about saving the ice-cream for later. It was too nice out, she said, and soon they'd be sailing into Glacier Bay. "Let's go out and watch for whales. Let's see glaciers birthing icebergs."

"They have the observation deck up front in operation again?"

She didn't answer. Maybe he hadn't said it in a way that was sufficiently question-inflected. He did that sometimes now, he knew, like his father—confused people, asking his questions in a way that sounded more like aggravated commentary.

"Your mother and I were out there all the first day until sunset. She really enjoyed that, I think, the drinks with the parasols and whatnot. Then they closed it for the weather. Mainly the wind, I think—afraid one of us would blow overboard. *Cattle overboard!* Has it been re-opened, do ya know? Maybe we should see if she wants to join us…"

Janelle continued tugging him along the hallway, bracing a hip against his now as she seized the door to the outside deck and threw all her weight into it. It was a stiffly hinged door with shiny windows and brass casements, hundreds of pounds too heavy. Herb should have rushed ahead of her to take care of that, but the moment was gone now.

"Leave it alone, Dad," she said.

"What's that now?"

"You know. Look, if she burns up a few grand in there, what's the big deal? It's not like you can't afford it. You think she doesn't deserve a little fun in life?"

That was it, in a nutshell—the whole problem with her and her generation: because he'd worked this hard to give her the life he hadn't had—one without financial hardship, and without a booze-smelling, malign old man in cowboy boots, practically a stranger, chasing you around the living room with his belt in a fist because he'd lost his paycheck on a horse named Pagan, or because he hadn't lost at all and he was just plain mean. She believed the packaging: if it said "Fun" on the label, then fun it was. Truth in advertising. Organic and pure meant just that, not *here's a new way to rip off the consumer*. Not a critical bone in her body. But he'd done that to her, because of the way he'd protected her, kept her safe and out of harm's way, except…but never mind that. You could do everything, but you couldn't keep death out.

Or maybe he had her all wrong. Maybe it was really the grief and sadness, the loss, always making her strive to prop *them* up and see the best in a situation, buoying them along. Maybe that was it and he was a jerk to think of her so critically. The cruise, after all, had been his idea, not hers, and a hard sell at that. So who was he to criticize? A floating fun factory: if ever there was a prescriptive forum for *fun to be had*, this was it, and he was the one who'd bought that particular BS hook, line, and sinker.

"Not *fun*, honey," he said. "It's a sickness. A disease. You wouldn't know. There's no fun in it."

But she wasn't listening and he found he'd lost the taste for saying it anyway. The words blew away in the humid Arctic air, stupid and meaningless though he'd meant them very much. There was just the dull hum of the ship going through the channel now, low like an enormous refrigerator; the rocky cliffs towering up out of the water over them, covered in mist-shrouded, wizened spruce and granite outcroppings; the sound of waves creaming the ship's sides way down there, six, seven stories down, and gulls crying. It had impressed him their first day on board, how quiet the ship was, and continued impressing him, now: drawn on by this humming, inexorable force, the thing just slid along. Huge and greasy and smooth. Below them, bobbing in the black green water displaced by their movement were the giant hunks of disfigured ice from the surrounding glaciers, which his daughter had mentioned: one like a giant skull, one like an embryo, clotted and stuck full of debris, sticks and branches, another, bigger, phosphorescent blue, with chunks of prehistoric rock scabbing its surface.

"Oh! Those are the old ones," she said, pointing. "The blue ones—they're super compressed, like, compacted over millions of years. Amazing, isn't it? Now they're melting. All of them, like the earth is shaking off its blankets."

He moved closer as if he were unable to hear or to follow what she was saying. Made some of his befuddled old man noises and wrapped an arm around her. He wondered if what had been making him feel so ragged and aggravated lately was not the ship or his wife after all; maybe something else—who could say what, something in his keister or his heart (same as the old man again) or liver, it didn't much matter—something was not right with him. Maybe he was dying. Like the old people who'd lived up here since forever and who would notoriously walk out onto the ice to die when they knew their game was up (he'd read about it; had heard the lectures from the naturalists in the Neptune Lounge, too)—the Natives—he was getting ready to go. That was why he'd brought them here. He held his breath now not to have to say anything about it. Withdrew his arm and felt her hair blow over his face, her fingers following quickly with a tinkling laugh like music, to tug the hair back and over one shoulder.

He wanted to give this moment more of his attention—to really fuse what his daughter was saying with the magnificent, bleak landscape, take it in and apply it to this sudden realization that he might be dying soon—but immediately, he was being distracted. There was an older man, almost his likeness, in a blue windbreaker at the railing beside him, taping the scene onto video, and chattering away authoritatively to his wife about whales and eagles while she stored frames on a digital camera which Herb recognized as being almost the same as his but higher priced and made by a different company (the zoom feature wouldn't work as well, he comforted himself by remembering, even if it had better storage and some fancy image manipulation functions his lacked). He'd thought hard about buying that very camera but had opted, in the end, for the half-priced one next to it—felt it'd been a real steal. Now he wondered. Wanted to strike up a conversation with them to check it out, compare notes, natter on a while about different options and specifics and share with them some of his new insights into the pleasures of electronic photography—how it could turn a hack like him into an artist, or something like it. How easy it was zapping a poor shot out of existence, re-framing a half-decent one, and how his computers at home were now bloated with shots he would never previously have considered himself capable of taking. *I used to think it was all luck*, he might have said. *Point the camera, see what you get. But no. It's trickery combined with skill—probably more trickery than skill, actually. Granted, some things are just never destined to be in a frame...*

"Let's move on," he said. "The cattle are lowing. Must be close to another feeding time."

"Dad." She ducked her head in a way he found endearing if a bit infuriating. She was tough as nails, his girl. No one would ever get to boss her around—not easily anyway. "Sure. Up or down?"

"Back. Let's sit on those little chairs on the poop deck and get us some blankets and martinis. How's that sound?"

She grinned and nudged him into motion.

But on the poop deck he was seized with the same melancholy. The vista opened out behind the ship, flat, waveless, desolate, the surface of the water where they'd passed stretching miles behind them in the channel, as far as he could see, like a scar. Like the water had been polished. So, their passage was not trackless. Of course— anything but. All of it was an illusion, the closeness with nature as well as the luxury, and yet sure enough, here they were. The cliffs ran straight into the water, rock-strewn and icy, and behind that it was all purple and mauve.

"Chowder," he said. "Forget the martini, I want some of that fish chowder and a hot chocolate. You?"

BACK IN THEIR STATEROOM, dressing for dinner (*formal* that night, Margo had reminded him scoldingly, and then asked for help with her pearls and the clasp at the back of her dress before swerving around him, clucking her tongue at his lateness, and slipping into the bathroom for a final touchup), he realized it wasn't the ship making him hate himself, any more than it was the booze that made him talk. He'd always hated himself, and always would, and he would always be a braggart. It was who he was. The one thing caused the other, though he could not explain or control this any better than he could say why he had never been one to play the ponies. He was watching himself in the stateroom mirror—gold and rose-tinted glass, and yet somehow supremely, exactingly unflattering—tucking in the tails of his dinner shirt and then stretching his arms up a moment so the shirt wouldn't accentuate his gut any more than it had to; watching his same old tired, sandy-red eyebrows going up and down in his forehead, his dead daughter's copper eyes, as he thought chidingly about the ship, the morons on the ship and how the whole experience had transformed Margo into this righteous betting hussy, when the realization hit him. *Another little fucking Polack Napoleon.* He had to sit a moment at the foot of their bed to register it, the rich scented air spewing from the overhead vent and tickling the few hairs at the top of his head. He was a fool and a braggart; that was him; and what he hated about everyone else on this ship was that he was no better than any of them—including, and most importantly, Margo.

Still they would fight before dinner, he knew it. He'd make some caustic remarks about her slots-playing, directly or indirectly, and she'd snipe back at him about his father and his brother and about being a kill-joy. Why had he married her?

She came out of the bathroom now and the whole room seemed to tilt out of kilter suddenly, to sway up creakingly, out of joint like an accordion, and back again. "Oh," she said, and eyed the ceiling. "We must be out of the channel."

"The high seas," he said. "Yes." Glanced at his watch. "Right on time. The cattle will be barfing up their dinners shortly."

The room plunged again and she took a few staggering steps to sit beside him. "Oh my. You have the nausea bands?"

"I'm good now, honey. Got my sea legs." Slapped his hands on his knees.

"I think you should put on a patch, or the bands. And I'm saying that for my own benefit as much as anyone else's." She leaned behind him to pull back the blind covering the window by their bed and peered out. She'd put on some new scent he noted—citrus and rose. He turned to look as well, but it was nothing to behold. Just a sheet of monochromatic grays out there. A dimly swaying gray horizon. Outside, he knew, waves would be bashing the stern and starboard side of the ship, wind kicking spray all the way up over the promenade deck; in here it just felt like your head had come slightly unscrewed. The chandeliers in the dining room would be swaying and the musicians would sound even more to his afflicted ears like a couple of windup toys.

"I'm telling you—I've got my sea legs. I'm good to go. You ready?"

"Where's Janelle?"

"She said she'd meet us—not to wait."

"Just don't say I didn't warn you. My years of cleaning up other peoples' sick and piss and shit are done, you know."

"Noted, dear."

"As if."

"Come on. Cocktail hour on the high seas," he said. He stood and offered her his hand. He'd done it. He hadn't said a single thing, straight or crooked, about the slots. He'd acted like it wasn't even there.

"Don't you want my latest accounting?"

"Couldn't care less," he said. "If it's…"

"Do I have the right state-room, here? Hel-low?" She lifted a hand over her eyes like a visor and squinted inquiringly at him. "Is that you, Herbie?" She had on the topaz and gold ring he'd bought her for their engagement. A huge rock, but no diamond. And the other one he'd bought her for their twentieth. In fact, her hand was almost covered in gaudy rings he'd bought for her in celebration of one occasion or another.

He shrugged. "It's your money as much as mine."

"Even if I maxed out all our credit cards?"

He drew a sharp breath. Felt his pulse sting a tick too quickly into his temples, constricting his vision. "You'd be singing a different tune. Come on. Let's go."

Still, she wouldn't take his hand. "I'm surprised." From this angle he could see into her cleavage, the pearls riding the powdered V of her flesh, and it occurred to him that really, for a woman in her fifties, she was doing all right. Her shoulders had a nice muscularity to them, and the skin wasn't too far gone. Good arms, too, and both tits still. He should count himself lucky.

"I can be a nice guy, too," he said.

"Should I bring my shawl?"

"That's up to you. I'd take a turn around the deck together, if that's what you're after."

She gave him the quizzical look he knew could as easily denote trouble ahead as it might presage some quirkily affectionate remark. "Well, whatever you took to improve your mood today, get some more of it."

"Viagra," he said and let a measured moment of silence elapse. "Just kidding. Actually, I think I might..."

"Don't," she said. She stood now, hand fiercely on his arm. "No more sarcasm. Just let's try and enjoy things a little."

"But I..."

"Don't say it!"

But at dinner, again, he was seized with hatred he didn't control. First it was Janelle and Margo, ribbing him about money he'd lost six years ago on a junk-bond deal involving fictitious sewage treatment plants in Yuma. How much had he lost there anyway? Come on, tell! Wasn't his fault, though, it was his investor's, the crook. The hack. No matter, one of the women at the table, seated across from him—a young, Irish thing, with freckles and elfin features that bothered him somehow (he couldn't say why, too happy and cheerful, maybe, too mindlessly self-assured, not long-suffering enough), and a dress cut to show the entire outline of her elfin breasts—had segued from that to the waste water contamination problem in *her* hometown (where was it? He couldn't even remember now—back East some place). Then it hit him: not two tables away and eating his dinner as calmly as any other guest on board, was the man, the *exact same* man, who'd run his daughter off the road fourteen years ago while driving drunk. They were at a new table this evening, right at the back of the banquet hall and up against the huge, sloping glass panels that looked out over the rear of the ship, or else Herb never would have noticed. He became aware of the man first in the reflection: his shoulders and the back of his head, the square cut of his black toupee against his shirt collar and his pink ears sticking out. And then, turning in his seat, to be sure, the whole familiar sight of him. Yes. Flat nose, like a boxer's, and the burst veins in his cheeks, pugnacious eyes in their swollen Asian folds, crooked little yellow teeth. It was him all right. The man had not aged a day somehow, nor had he been ruined by the heartache of guilt, or by the court settlement which had ostensibly stripped him penniless and put him in jail the last twelve and a half years. How was it possible? He'd survived. He was out again on parole, maybe, and still drinking, two tables away. What were the odds?

"Margo," he hissed. Dropped a hand to her leg and squeezed, hard. "Look!"

But she wouldn't remove her attention from the young girl. Not right away, at least. Shifted her leg to the side and pushed back, just as hard, with the back of her hand, gemstones cutting him.

"Yes," she said, finally. Turned to face him, lip drawn back, lipstick smearing one of her front teeth. "Yes, dear. What is it?"

"It's him—it's that Donald Li-Chin guy. Right there." He jerked his head. "*Look!*"

For one moment, he thought, she seemed sufficiently horrified.

Then she was laughing at him, doubled over and tittering, a hand to her mouth. How much of his money had she burned up that day, anyway? She'd said it a moment ago and he'd blanked it out—had purposely made himself not hear. A lot. For a moment he almost couldn't distinguish his anger and grief about that from what he felt for Li-Chin. "My dear, he's *incarcerated*, it can't be…"

"I'm telling you! Look again."

"Honey. That man's Hispanic. Chin was an Oriental."

"*Li*-Chin. You can't even say his name right."

Soup came, and salad, and more bread, and appetizers, main courses, more wine, still he kept watching the man in the reflection. The back of his head, his jaws working. Him. It had to be. Every few minutes to confirm it he'd turn all the way around in his seat and stare, as if inviting the man into a confrontation, asking him to come over and say anything, apologize, refute him. Same nose, same eyes, same pocked and dented cheeks. It was him all right.

"Why don't you go introduce yourself, Herb. You're staring enough, it's getting a little embarrassing."

"I'd like to go over and bash his God damn head in, is what."

"That's a bottle of wine and three bloody marys talking. What is it you always say? *Sure love the taste of alcohol but I don't much like to listen to it?* There's no Chin on this boat! OK? Get it through your head." She flicked a nail at his temple, not softly. "Better yet, like I said, go ask him. Introduce yourself. See what he says." Then, to the woman beside her, "Herbie here's convinced that man over there killed our daughter."

He saw himself in the glass, leaning up from his seat and sinking back again: pink spots on his cheeks just under the eyes, and the horrible stinginess, the mean old-man stingy greed in his eyes that said always *more, more, I want more* (so it wasn't ego after all, just plain old greed) and which that actor had cleverly enough excluded from his televised presentation/imitation of Herb, had supplanted with nutty, zealous magnanimity, the kind to make you think *crazy price cuts, lucky deals*, not *murderer*. Not *crook*. "Zack, crazy Zack," he muttered. No, he wasn't crazy like that. He wouldn't hurt a flea. He had both hands on the edge of the table now, table cloth bunched in his fists. Behind him they were singing something—sounded like the national anthem, only different, higher and faster, out of tune, waiters carrying flaming baked Alaskas down the runway, blue ones meant to look like ancient glaciers on fire, and waving sparklers around their heads. July 4th—was it July 4th already? He closed his eyes and tried not to hear it. Tipped back against the ship's motion, and braced his hands flat on the table. Felt his gorge rising. It wasn't Li-Chin over there. Couldn't be. Except that it *was*. He looked again. It was him all right.

"Excuse me a moment," he said, and pushed back out of his seat—taste of garlic in his throat now, wine drying his mouth and sinuses, and pressing into his larynx with the bread and salad and stroganoff and garlic mashed potatoes and lobster chowder and roasted peppers and pickled oysters and cheese soufflé and... "Off to the gents." The floor tilted as if to accommodate him, and in two steps, three more, lunging with the ship, he was at the other table, towering over him. He was seeing them both in the glass and backlit by the Arctic twilight, not quite black, not quite gray, the endless sunset—the little pink spot on his chin now gleaming and raw as a bull's-eye, shining with spittle—then seeing the man again straight on and knowing, suddenly, it was not him after all. He was horribly mistaken. The man peered up at him, eyebrows lifting, ready with his own questions and counter-accusations, bringing those from behind the screen of puzzled worry and politeness into words: *Do I know you? Have you lost something?*

Who are you?

THE BOWMAKER'S CATS

WE'D BEEN TO THE BOWMAKER'S HOUSE before, but not recently, and never all of us together. We'd toured his workshop and house, seen his shelves of stacked bow blanks, his grove of aged Pernambuco logs lain horizontally in the basement, his ebony stumps for frogs and store of mastodon tusks for tips, his drawers of abalone shell, whale baleen, bits of lizard skin, and hanks of Mongolian stallion tail hair. His knives and planes and gouges and buffing pads and leathers. We'd watched him at work pedaling his antique jeweler's lathe, shorn gold filings piled on the floor around him. Watched him heat a straight length of faceted Pernambuco in the alcohol lamp and gently pry it back to the exact leg-bone curve in which it would serve the rest of its life. Lined up and hairless in his downstairs window rack to sun-cure, those bows were candy in the brain: sounds to imagine and not yet hear. Perfect, therefore, and better (maybe; almost) to look at than to play. Perfect, too, in the way we could imagine them responding in our hands—exactly mated to the finger's asymmetry, perfectly weighted and balanced, pressure of thumb on the thumb grip, forefinger cocked against the silk and gold winding. Zing! To see one was to ache to hear and play it. Pull, press, draw it down and back and down again across the strings. Listen. Glide the sound out. Polished as gems, shapelier than roots or bones or antlers, but somehow calling these things to mind (also: lager, absinthe, amber single malt in a glass, the outer wrappings of a cigar, sun on a summer wheat field).

Aside from bows that didn't play themselves or otherwise make a sound, and the career-sized store of supplies to make them, the bowmaker had in his possession three invisible cats and a wife whom no one, in all the times we'd visited, had ever seen or spoken to. We'd heard tell of her and were mostly assured of her existence—there were the signs, certainly, even if she wasn't physically present: special foods in small dishes left lying around on the dining room table; the smaller, shorter workbench adjacent to his where she did her rehairs and high-dollar restorations; the jackets, sweaters, shawls, worn-out party shoes and hats, all vaguely retaining a delicate female form, some lightly soiled, and left hanging over the backs of chairs and from hooks and doorknobs and on the dusty downstairs coat rack. She might have been a beauty. Raven-haired or red-haired with a sullen glare and a widow's peak. Or mild and gentle as the surrounding countryside and fall wheat fields. We weren't sure. There was a sorrowful past attached to her—this we knew from our leader who'd been told it by the bowmaker himself: something involving a foreign prince, and fleet of stolen Audis, and backwards squirrel-hunting parents who had long ago disowned her.

He was always talking, the bowmaker. He did not meet eyes, exactly, as he talked, but blinked and rolled his eyes up into his head or cast his gaze away somewhere a few inches to the right or left of us, observing a spot on the wall maybe, stroking his beard and mustache downward with the skillful, blunt-tipped fingers that were his whole livelihood, in preparation of answering (at length) our questions. And as he talked, the more he talked and talked, we were persistently aware that one of his teeth was rotten—hidden there inside his head, somewhere, and undeniably rotten. Possibly abscessed. The smell of it, heavy, boozy, like rotten cabbage or sausage, some kind of funky old meat, stampeded us in wafts, solid-seeming with the humidity of his breath and spit and other odors having to do with the digestion of his lunch. The direction, timing, and relative velocity of his exhalations were not easy to predict—each one's movement unseeable in the surrounding air: try as we might, angling heads and shifting back a step or to the side, the occasional full-face collision with one was inevitable. In this manner all of his meanings and explanations, his lengthy asides and answers became imbued for us with a vague dread and nauseated embarrassment and unwelcome reminder of boiled fish.

We were there, of course, for the bows. To try them, to play them, with the intent, naturally, of purchasing one or two, if the price was right. We had not abandoned our shoes in a heap at his front door to wander his house and workshop sock-footed while he went on about his secret cats or the invisible woman he called his wife. But the more he explained things, the more we wondered. Planes, finger planes, lathes, knives, glues, jigs, clamps, lamps, drawers of shell and gold and tortoise shell and pretty metric screws…with each tool and process laid bare, each variety of wood and exotic material shown in its original, harvested state, we felt increasingly concerned about the things not said. All these years he'd worked reducing his production needs to mimic the most ancient, time-honored bowmaking methods and practices (mostly French, of course): no power tools or artificial lights, no virtual mock-ups, no petroleum products. Yes. But why were there bowls of cat food and water dishes left standing by the door and no cats anywhere? Why the smell of cat piss and no cats? Where did they hide? Where was his wife?

He had just finished explaining the procedure for engraving the nipple end of a gold thumbscrew and was now tilting back on his stool, chin in hand, fingers probing externally the area of his rotten tooth, and ready at last to consider one of our "off-topic" questions: "About the cats. Yes. They're just terribly shy. As soon as they hear a person, a human voice that's not mine, they hide under the house. But they're here all right, believe me. You just won't see them." We wanted more, of course. How had they become so shy? Were they always shy? If so, how had they come to be owned by a man as loquacious as the bowmaker? Had his wife played some part in their emotional conversion? Had she played with them, period? Was she with them now, perhaps, under the house, playing? But he would not indulge our interests any further. "See here," he said, turning slightly to reach and pluck down a bow from the rack overhanging his wife's smaller bench: an item of rarest antiquity, sent from Tokyo for new hair—French with a sloping tip, and an ivory frog restored years ago, ostensibly by his invisible wife. "Soft as a noodle," he said, gently mashing the tip in one palm to make the stick move for us, waggle side to side. "Don't try that at home. Rubbery. But this is an amazing bow! Pernambuco like this…it actually doesn't exist anymore, except on the black market. Demands a whole different playing style and method of construction, see? Supple! People, some people, particularly classical players in the romantic style, adore it."

Note, we did not ask how much: more money than all of us together earned in a year; more than we'd ever see in one place at one time. That much we knew. The actual amount was inconsequential. Note, too, we are none of us classical players in the romantic style. We've studied it, of course, some more than others and found it mostly doesn't agree with us. That is, it agrees with us as much as any other style or form of music one hears in passing and hums along with, studies briefly, snapping fingers, but afterwards can't remember. Our preference is for the music which conceals in its expression an emotion so powerful that to state it more directly would be to destroy and contaminate it with *drama*, driving away the listener—so: more restrained classical and baroque (Bach, say, but not Monteverdi), music of the late Renaissance, Gregorian chant, Monk, Mingus, Miles, some bluegrass, Nick Drake, music of the Mongolian prairies, etc. Again he caressed the tip of the bow, enfolding more and more of the stick in his palm, back halfway to the thumb grip, laughing softly to himself almost as if he were aroused by a lover, he pressed down with his other hand and made it wiggle. "See the flexion! But if you can get used to it, the tone to be had from a bow like this is actually…incomparable! The last one I saw at Sotheby's auctioned for, oh, let's say high six figures. This one's been appraised at slightly less than that because of the, uh, the restoration. An important bow, but not as historically significant as it might be—as others like it."

Again he turned, this time with a hint of rage in his expression—professional jealousy? anxiety?—some of us were able to observe this in the window, which reflected his profile from the neck up, others had to infer it from the sudden squaring of his shoulders and blusterously delicate but undeniably dismissive manner of re-hanging the bow by its tip on the rack overhanging his wife's workbench.

"So, next," he said, continuing with his step-wise explanation of the process of making a violin bow. The oversized octagonal rough shape, the paring away of wood, the constant stress testing, the fitting of the frog; the floor around him was littered with little red curls and chips and shavings of rarest heartwood…

But we'd seen it all now. We were ready to play. Only playing, we thought, would make certain things clear again.

Into the testing room we went—not so much a room as a partially renovated in-law apartment of plasterboard and wainscot with strategically suspended head-sized foam wedges and larger baffles, one wall draped in old sleeping bags, all of it arranged not to distort or enhance any single frequency with reflective junk sound. Here again he was in his element and ready to demonstrate for us, stamping his slippered feet, grunting, laughing, clapping hands, clearing his throat, positioning and repositioning baffles so we understood the care he'd taken constructing this perfectly flat, sonic environment: "The only reflective surfaces here…and here, this little bit of floor, and of course some of the ceiling, over there…will give you an overall ambient sound not uncharacteristic of a small concert hall. If we move the baffles you can change that, of course, to your liking, but most people prefer starting here. Kind of the default position. Maybe a bit on the dry side. But honest. It's an honest sound, not too many overtones, a lot of fundamental. It won't hide a thing."

Note, too, we are experts in what we do, but we are not snobs. We are not fanatics desperate to impose our sensitivities or beliefs on the rest of the world. Most of our adult lives we've devoted to the art (the skill? the practice?) of purifying pitch and sonority by the movement of fingers sometimes less than fractions of a millimeter, the better or more exactly to convey our thought and feeling in a musical line and drive a spike through the listener's heart. Our lives are ruled equally by the infitesimal and the grand: a milligram of wood shaved from a bridge, a soundpost tapped and squeezed fewer than .2 millimeters closer to the foot of a bridge, a fingernail pared to make the note intonate closer to perfection, a fleck of gold in our rosin. We don't think twice about any of this. No, we think continually about all of it. Habitually. To the point it no longer really matters. Fellow travelers on airplanes count numbers and study golf manuals, consult the pros on how to adjust the positioning of a thumb or hip or foot inches one way or the other to improve the swing or the putt; we fine-tune the microscopes of our souls to register hair's-breadth adjustments, which no one but us will ever hear, exactly, but all the best of our listeners will know and feel profoundly. We are none of us fussy or delicate people. We like what we do. We also like cooking and driving fast, building stone walls, skiing with our children, chopping down trees, and hunting small animals, as time allows. Most of us, more than anything, long to be loved. In this, as well, we want the bowmaker's help. With his help, we think (we hope), we will play that much more productively, with a warmth and purity of tone no one in his right mind will be able to resist.

First up, of course, our leader chooses the bow we'd all known he would choose to start with: the dark, sexy-girl one, with a sloping, striated head and clear grain (from a stock of wood the bowmaker once was overheard calling his "Pecatte wood")—grain you can see so deeply into it is like seeing through a piece of cheese. No, like looking into a rushing, frozen trout stream and seeing all the muddy and whiskery sun-streaked levels of it revealed simultaneously. No, like… Anyway, he is hastily unbuttoning his old case, flicking the strings of his violin to check his tuning, wiping away old rosin. And then the moment: he's as delighted in the seconds preceding it as in the seconds we're sure will follow, as sound enwraps the room and the violin sings beyond its heretofore recognized potential, the notes wider, deeper, harder, warmer and more natural, nestling to a fundamental of pitch never before heard. We know it's coming. We see it in his face, mild, astonished as a man about to experience religious conversion; he studies the bow a last time, caressing it in the palm of his right hand and polishing the ferrule on his shirttail, seeing the lamp-lit glow of the abalone eye and slide wink on and off at him from the perfect black of the frog as he tilts it in and out of the light. He is pleased, he is so pleased, he is ready...

The door bursts open and the bowmaker strides back into the room, clearing his throat. He seems nervous, ill at ease, anyway, which is to say his manner seems now more abrupt and sudden than previously (and in a way to remind some of us of the weight and shape and heft of particular knives and gouges on his bench two doors down). Had he left the room? When did he leave the room? Did any of us notice? To reenter the room he must have left it, requiring us to presume either a hole in our perceptions, a gap in time, or some kind of hypnotized mind-meld-like group-hallucination in which all of us ceased noticing his all-too-noticeable movements in and around a room. No explanation seems adequate to the problem of his sudden removal from and reentry into the room. Regardless, we must accept it, recognizing, as we do, that he is no longer exactly who he'd been before leaving the room and reentering it. He is larger and less ideal-seeming. Reddened. He has lost something and gained something else back in its place. His mood, anyway, is much changed, and we are no longer sure we will hear him as well (which is to say as impartially, notwithstanding his breath and the need for positioning your head to escape its full impact). But like it or not, we will have to hear him.

"The Pajeot," he says. He says it in an accusatory manner.

Yes, some of us say.

We can try it as well, sure.

You want us to play it?

I'd love to!

We'll be glad to put it in the mix.
Strictly for laughs.
Do you have a spare few hundred thousand dollars?
Heh. Very funny.
It's not even for sale though, is it?

"The Pajeot," he repeats. He shakes his head and his tone—like none of us has spoken: "The Pajeot is gone. No one has been in this shop all afternoon. No one has come in or out of that front door since you all arrived. Which means one of you, someone amongst you, has that bow. Now," here again he cast his gaze somewhere beyond us and then, with a fluttering of eyelids, rolled both eyes up into his head and continued, eyelids faintly thrumming. "Now, I'm going to leave you gentlemen alone and will trust that between the six of you—pardon, the eight of you—you can learn what's happened and return the bow to my wife's bench, no questions asked." That he was moved by the disappearance of his (so-called) wife's high stakes rehair job was evident enough to us without getting a direct look into his eyes for confirmation. Some of us, all the same, peered up after him at the ceiling, in empathy, perhaps, or in the vain hope of seeing reflected there, in whatever he was studying, the root source of his agitation while others stood slightly on tiptoe to catch a first glimpse of tears (or any other outward manifestation of a distraught emotional condition) and thereby to guess what it was to be him and so troubled by vanishing cats and wives and now bows. Maybe it was just a very shy bow? Maybe at the first sound of any other bows it hid under the house? None of us pointed out his errors in counting our number and gender, though one of us did clear her throat delicately, perhaps confessionally, forcefully enough, anyway, to draw some attention to herself, breathing in once as if she were about to pounce on a topic or own up to the theft (or to being his lost wife?), but no words came. No one said a thing. "So then," he repeated, "I was hoping it'd be easier than this, but apparently it isn't. Umm. So, like I said, I'll just leave you gentlemen here to sort it out and will be downstairs awaiting your, uh, call." And with that he withdrew.

A word or two about the bowmaker's house is probably in order. Rambling without being huge; three stories with a semiattached root cellar (wherein his store of ebony stumps, mastodon tusks and Pernambuco logs lay, as well as a pallet of recently acquired Makassar ebony fence posts, purest heartwood of old growth, perfectly preserved and bought directly from Africa). Under the house, a crawl space more dungeon than cellar. Rooms and rooms, most half-finished, some nicely furnished, all with high ceilings, and painted pine wood floors. Rectangular windows of notable height, all rattly in their casings and, at this time of year, covered in plastic insulating wrap. A sweltering smell of cat piss boiling up from all floorboards, everywhere. In-law apartments upstairs and downstairs and one extending from the semiattached root cellar. Partially finished attic with moaning eaves, no insulation, and again, smells of feral cat. More bowls of cat food and wainscot walls in terrible disrepair. In short: any number of rooms, nooks, crannies, closets, trunks, cabinets, standing wardrobes, any number of *places* for a hiding bow, wife, and several cats. A house which could conceal easily as much as it revealed, and very possibly a good deal more.

Once he'd gone we looked inquiringly at one another, but still no one said anything. Our leader, who had been so ready to play only moments ago, now appeared defeated and dazed. He appeared as many of us had (and often) at other times in our lives, and as many of us had seen others in our group looking, in moments of worst disappointment and upset: like a man who would never play the violin again. He was holding his instrument against his shoulder, still plucking faintly at the strings with his left fingertips, the bow pointing at the ground and dangling from his right forefinger, but all of it, his violin and the bow, seemed returned to its original dumb and just-harvested state. A hunk of pretty and shaped hollow wood, spruce and book-matched maple; a strip of bent Pernambuco with horse hair uncompromisingly attached at its tip and frog for no purpose, and dusted with rosin. He looked, in a word, *miserable*. And seeing that in him, that appearance of most corpse-like despondent purposelessness, we did what we always do in these situations—what we are schooled to do. We mustered our strength and gave encouragement. We did so scoldingly, according to form and instinct. We said, "Pah! That's a fine-looking bow there. Play it! Play us some nice music already! Get over yourself. Come on!" He resisted at first, but he was schooled in this resistance too (to test us and himself), and was inclined, anyway, by nature to accept praise and comforting words eventually, at least halfway. All part of the game, part of our livelihood: play on even through death and tragedy and every size of misfortune. The show goes on! Play even when you know it's miserable and your fingers are cold and stiff and sore, and the thing sounds like a wire nailed to an old board and nothing works the way you know it should and will eventually. Willpower! Overcome the inert with your art and make it live again. He shook his head, but we knew already we were winning; we saw his eyes brightening, becoming alert again and more reflective of the surrounding light, blinking in anticipation of fine new things. We saw him considering the possibilities of the bowmaker's bow, of all his bows, and then counting the others arrayed on the table before us—gold and silver and one with a tortoise-shell frog. Had they multiplied since the bowmaker's abrupt second exit from the room? Or were our mathematical abilities failing as well? We were sure there had been four bows; now it seemed as if there were five, counting the one in our leader's hand. We saw him tilt it again to admire the abalone lights in the slide and the eyes of the frog, shaking his head with wonderment. "Yes," we said. "Play!"

But we couldn't hear him. Not at first, anyway. Maybe in his zeal to arrange the room to cancel junk frequencies, the bowmaker had actually wiped out *all* frequencies relating to the sound of a violin. Maybe by repositioning some foam wedges, pushing back baffles and undraping walls, we'd regain our hearing? There he was, our leader, arm pumping, fingers twirling, and giving us his usual deadpan look of joyous sorrow as he tore into it—his *staring down the gods expression*, as one reviewer called it—biting his lips and swinging his head, but no sound: nothing reached us. Maybe we'd spent so long hearing the bowmaker's stories and explanations his voice was now stuck in our heads, overwhelming our senses to the point that no music could get in: his tales of early violin-building school days, fencing old classmates, naked, with hairless junker bows out in the quad; coed badminton games featuring the use of junk violins as racquets; and, of course, his explanations of all the processes: "If I cut this way the run-out's not as bad, see, and I might get a viola bow here, and another violin bow over there. But I can't go *here*. That check *there*, that's the dead spot. The rotten spot. Though you never really know…well, you have a pretty good idea, anyway—certainly by this time, I have a pretty good idea, eyeballing a blank, what'll work best but there's always surprises …" So on and so on. We covered our ears and uncovered them. Nothing.

Done, our leader was now recounting his initial impressions and, to our surprise, not only did we hear him, his voice had become nearly identical to the bowmaker's. Was it general proximity to the bowmaker that threatened erasure or transformation for all things—bows, cats, wives, *voices?* Was everything he touched or talked about or liked subject to being changed into something else? Was his personality so pervasive as to infect everything it contacted? "That's stirring up a lot of sound there! Good high frequencies, not at all unpleasing. I'm not completely, one-hundred percent over the top sold on it, but oh, maybe…I *like* it. What do you think? Any of you? Thoughts? Let's try…how about…" He did not roll his eyes up or look anywhere but directly at us or the bows as he spoke. Still, we were sure it was not his voice we heard but some ventriloquized imitation of the bowmaker's. Already he had the next selection in hand and was eagerly tapping its tip in his palm, smiling dog-like, ready to begin. "Why so quiet all of a sudden? Come on. This," he paused to glance again and nod his head. He moved a few steps closer, shouldering aside baffles to clear a new space for himself. "This one, I have a good feeling about it. It might be the one. Look!"

If only the bowmaker would return, we thought. If only he were here so his voice would be his own again, not superimposed on our leader, and so we'd have his descriptions and explanations once more, and everything would be back to normal.

But now our leader was playing, and as he did, all of our wishes, along with our various forms of doubt and confusion, vanished. A favorite of his—the Bach Chaconne. It was him, all right: his voice and style underlying the tone, his particular muscle and brio, everything about him intact. There was even his usual mistake of forcing some of the downbeats, pushing just a little more heavily than necessary, so a kind of too-aggressive, swaggering posture overlaying the music. And maybe, some of us now saw, maybe this was how he'd come to be our leader in the first place: it was the stance of authority we followed because we *needed* to believe in it as badly as he needed it there to keep concealed whatever was back there, inside it, hidden—whatever he'd been keeping from us and from himself all these years. For a second some of us thought we were really able to see it, too—the rotten, vanquished, half-enervated little thing strutting around under cover of his big-man too-much-bluster style—and then, like that, it was gone. The *music* had taken it, concealed and transformed it, lifting him right along, soaring out of himself to where he alone (among us, anyway) could go, technically speaking, and reminding us, as he went, of everything *else* he'd also always been and why he was our leader: the boy genius, the man with the tone, the *one* with a direct line to the main force behind the music. There was nothing new or different here; nothing changed: it was just him, but that much clearer.

Well, someone said.

Hot dog, that sounded all right.

That's a bow.

You have to have that bow.

I'm not so sure.

Oh, I'm sure. It's you.

WE NEVER SAW THE BOWMAKER AGAIN, not that day, not ever. To our knowledge his bows, aside from the ones for which we left payment—one silver, one gold, one gold and tortoise with a very French tip—are all still at his house, on his bench, in his window, or in the upstairs in-law "sound chamber" apartment, hairs slackened off so as not to wreck the camber of the stick, all of them waiting to be owned and played. They are fine but voiceless and not, ultimately, for our purposes, as fine as other bows, given our particular setups and playing styles. Not all bows and instruments are equal. This is a fact of life. Not all bows sound equally good on all instruments. The bows that speak in our hands and on our instruments: we love them. We cannot live without them. The others, Pajeots, Pecattes, whoever else, where they end up is no concern to us. Nor is it our concern where the bowmaker went. We did not kill him or in any other way harm him or cause him to vanish, nor did we steal anything of his. He does not return phone calls; our checks to him have long since expired; his stores of wood and other bowmaking tools and supplies have not shown up, to our knowledge, at auction or on any black markets. We've seen new bows of his for sale, sometimes, but no one can say if these are straight off his bench or older stock held back in some dealer's storeroom for years. The youngest among us, for a while, worried about the cats. Would they be all right without him? If he was gone, were they gone as well, or stuck eternally under his house? Invisible still? Some contemplated an exploratory break-in—call it a rescue mission—until we reminded them, this is the nature of cats (and apparently bows and bowmakers too), and always has been: they do not *need*, generally, and certainly don't need *us*. Visible, invisible, shy, not shy, it is about the only thing we can say for sure about them: they persist. They may, in fact, prefer persisting in solitude, unseen. Or not. Who knows? And this is only one of many things in the endlessly bowed and expanding universe we will never understand.

A BEAR FOR TRYING

HE JUST NEEDED TO GET RID of all the little animals super-glued to his dashboard. It wouldn't be easy. Some of the figures were glass or china, and the ones that weren't looked to be made of some kind of dense plastic. He could envision the wreckage it would leave, the miniature china legs snapped off and mired in glue, presenting a hazard for children (not that he knew many)—for all people, really, reaching in the dark—the plastic ones tearing away chunks of dashboard vinyl and paint or else leaving behind pieces of themselves like some kind of alien gumbo. So he waited. Mornings, starting on his way into work, he'd see them there, impervious to all weather and temperature changes, with their stupid fixed expressions of pleasant neutrality, nothing like real animals—a deer and fawn, cow, pig with a peg-leg, sheep, mother bear, two squirrels, an eagle and a rabbit—and he'd remember all of his conviction to deal with them, soon, possibly even over the weekend. Chisels and sandpaper. Some kind of solvent too, he supposed, though he'd need to research that first, call his buddy Fred at the Ford dealership and endure his jokes—*Finally decided to quit playing Noah's fucking ark, huh?*—to find out which brands might do the least harm. And then stuck at stop lights, the way people would glance at him and glance again, smiling nervously sometimes, bobbing their heads, but also occasionally laughing and pointing, some days it was all he could do to keep himself from just bashing a hand down on the whole menagerie to make it go away—diabolical, reverse genesis. But aside from the mess and potential lowered resale value on his truck, potential need to replace the whole dash (not something he could afford just now), as well as the real risk of cutting his hand in the process, something in one of the animals' expressions always stopped him—something pathetic and harmless that reminded him of all pathetic, harmless things. And though his brother might at times have seemed deserving of pity, Karl knew from experience that Eber was in fact anything *but* harmless or pathetic; still, he worried that if he did anything to uproot or deface the animals he might, by some unwitting force of voodoo, wreak havoc on Eber's situation. He'd read somewhere that the greater the level of uncertainty and instability in any person's life, the more likely that person was to find himself turning to these things like astrology, numerology, scientology, voodoo and the like. And he had to admit, with Eber gone, a certain something—call it stability, excitement, purpose—had gone missing in his life. So he gritted his teeth and held back. Parked in the farthest possible employee parking space, away from anyone else, locked and went across the parking lot to the paint store. As he went, he ran down one of a handful of familiar one-sided internal dialogues with Eber to rev himself up for the day ahead and put things in perspective—none of which changed the fact that Eber was gone now the last four and a half months, in California presumably with their mother, whose leaky heart beat three different ways the same as Eber's, no indication he'd ever be back, and all of this largely because of his own, Karl's, stupid behavior while Eber had been recovering in the heart wing. They'd thought he might be dying. Who knew?

Glimpsing himself in the glass of the shop door—beard, square-rim glasses, paint store company shirt, name stitched over the breast pocket—he'd remember the other promise he was always making himself and forgetting or pushing aside: get a gym membership at the yuppie twenty-four hour place up on 57th. Do some free weights and cardio. His heart might be steady and pinhole-free, unlike Eber's, but he wasn't doing himself any favors letting things slip this far. Once, they'd been potential college running backs, he and Eber. But most of the their high school years together they'd spent avoiding greatness, partying with the skater kids, cutting class and skipping practices to the brink of being benched for delinquency, polishing a dedication to remaining non-entities at any cost—alien kids, half-Jewish half-Mexican, all-un-American. Screw the world. That attitude wouldn't cut it for him anymore, if it ever had. He knew this. But with the smell of coffee on the heated air (and instantly he was picturing a fresh hot mug, three sugar packets shaken in, two creamers, single plain donut to start), soon enough he forgot everything else: the twenty-four hour place, California, Eber and Kelly, and all the stupid plastic and china animals glued to his dashboard. Put it all out of his mind until quitting time, when once again, dome light coming on, key going into the ignition, he saw the animals and remembered.

Years ago—fourteen, to be exact—eighteen years old and finally, legally of an age to commit stupid acts with no adult signature on the waiver form, he'd been the one first convinced of the significance in these parting-shot gestures of indelible truth and meaning. He had, consequently, blown most of his first month's pay from bagging groceries at the Safeway on a tattoo. He did it to piss off his father. To prove something about how independent-minded he'd grown and how he didn't need anyone's help or advice. Also, he'd wanted to prove to Eber that this *could* in fact be done—the old man could be stood down and argued out of his bullshit principles. In this way a new world could be had. But more immediately (and sadly, this was the only part that really mattered anymore because it was all that remained, inked in the skin on the back of his neck) he'd done it to prove once and for all how much he loved the girl he was then dating. Kimberly. So, a pair of dragon-scaled sturgeon encircling each other, head to tail, because it had something to do with her astrological sign or whatever, and also signified eternity while making a semi-private reference to their favorite sexual position. And for a while it really had pleased her—made her quit nagging for promises and false assurances. Long before the girlfriend drifted on, his old man had gotten over the tattoo and quit his smirking and *tsks* and disparaging remarks—*Your Ma is a Jew, Karl, remember that; you'll never get in the Jew cemetery now, not that you probably care much; never get a decent job either, not that you care much about that either, apparently, though perhaps someday you will...* Soon the old man seemed to forget the tattoo entirely. Nothing at all had been proven or changed. So he tried again. Anchors on either shoulder to commemorate a newfound passion for all things nautical. A Celtic knot on his heart following another breakup close on the heels of the overdose death of one of his good friends; that one was to signify his own complexity and the generally barbaric ass-backwardness of life, which, sad though it was, could also at times be beautiful in a heavy metal sort of way if you chose to see it like that. He tried and tried until he realized nothing could be proven or accomplished in this manner—no conviction or feeling inked under the skin lasted any longer than the ones you simply forgot about and let go. Meanwhile, he was turning himself into a circus freak, and to no apparent gain. He needed to stop, and did...after a final Caracara and rattlesnake tattoo in memory of their father, days before his and Eber's twenty-seventh birthday and just over a year after the old man's death. Done—no more tattoos. Thankfully, with his sleeves rolled down and collar buttoned to an inch of his neck-line he could still pass. He'd been smart enough or conservative enough to anticipate that—so, no tribal tats stamped up the neck, no facial designs or piercings, no four letter words across his knuckles.

The animal thing was much more recent, started this past summer with just the one cow, hooves in a puddle of Gorilla Super Glue in the middle of Karl's dash, because it did not in any way stand for or commemorate the thing he and Eber would always be reminded of seeing it, and because it was just plain hysterical. A single plastic cow on the dashboard. Unfortunately (Eber's idea) the Gorilla Super Glue had from then on lived in Karl's glove compartment, so for a time whenever he and Eber were out together and something struck them as commemoration-worthy, silly, remarkable, outrageous, up went another animal. Half of a summer and fall it was like that, a running joke and a way to challenge each other to non-greatness and epic stupidity—*a rabbit if you go ask that girl if she shaves her pussy; a camel if you get your dick in that girl by the end of the night, a bear for trying...* In retrospect, the point of it all had been some last-ditch effort to keep their days from seeming too much the same—a last ditch effort to revive youthful antics, stay forever young, shift the passage of time back to where it belonged, and forestall the inevitable a while longer. On it went, three months, four months, mainly Eber daring Karl, Karl complying, until the week the Gorilla Super Glue froze solid in Karl's glove compartment and a few days later, having unfrozen, oozed from the popped husk of itself over the maps and receipts and dead flashlights, spare headlight bulbs, registration, expired insurance cards, garter belt from a girl he'd been to a wedding with some years ago—glued all of it into a single lump of crap he could do nothing to salvage and was barely able to pry from the glove compartment. The same week, as it happened, Eber's heart quit beating long enough that the medics, reviving him, couldn't say for sure what kind of recovery he'd be looking at—whether or not he'd walk or talk or run again; whether he'd be back from the hospital, period. Karl was in line at the drive-through when Kelly called, stuck between SUVs in the single-lane conveyor belt of vehicle-bound customers awaiting tacos and soft-drink orders. He pounded on his steering wheel, leaned into his seat and pushed back on the steering wheel as hard as he could, as if that would help speed up his progress. *We gotta get there, Karl, one or both of us, gotta be there when he comes out of it! Holy fuck! If he does. He's not... I'm gonna hang up now and call Sharon from work. Maybe she can get here faster. You can meet me? It's Sacred Heart. ...Oh my god it was so surreal! One minute there he was jabbering away in the next room, you know how he is, talking tough, asking me about such and such at work, meridians and shit like that, and then... By the time I got to him he's just all cold and sweaty, laying there! Oh my god, Karl, you gotta get here.*

He knew there was nothing wrong with his own heart—nothing more wrong, anyway, than the usual damages a lifetime of smokes and uppers, pot, and bad diet might have inflicted—but that afternoon, waiting to make it out of the drive-through lane and across town to Kelly, and from there, seeing she was already gone, up the hill to Sacred Heart hospital, he'd been sure he must be experiencing some of Eber's heart trauma. A wobbly weakness and woozy flutteringness through all of his perceptions, acrid copper taste at the back of his throat to accompany it, almost like finishing a set of hard wind-sprints only without the endorphin-rush to make you feel equal parts omnipotent and nauseated. Just plain old old-man weak and wobbly. He wasn't too worried. Knew from previous experience he and Eber could at times share each other's dreams and highs and perceptions in a way normal people didn't—they had to be in the absolutely right frame of mind and surrendered to each other, dialed in at exactly the right frequency for it to happen, but it did. It happened. Once their dad had put them up for a week as paid test subjects at one of the teaching hospital-clinics in town—some kind of stress-testing related to identical twins—and they'd learned there some of what might or might not comprise a special brain-wave bond in the connection between them. So he wasn't too surprised or worried for himself, though he was plenty afraid for Eber. Things kept going soft-focus on him, the slowed passage of time making everything appear not quite there, not quite three-dimensional, and he was way too aware of his heart squeezing the blood along. Thu-thump, thu-thump. *Shoulda been me*, he thought the instant he saw Kelly there in the heart ward waiting room under the TV, bundled in her parka and too big scarf, fake Uggs crossed under her on the dingy plastic of the waiting area couch, though it was still early November and, cold snap aside, not that winter-like out yet, talking on her cell phone. And when she looked up at him, *They got the wrong brother. Should have been Karl, not Eber*—like he was somehow momentarily intercepting all of *her* thoughts as well now. Though he knew, likely as not in such distressed situations, intercepted thoughts could be all wrong, easily misread and scrambled, the way she threw herself at him, hot, radiant, crying into his jacket collar, for better or worse things were now on the verge of a change.

Way early on, five-six years ago, not long after Kelly and Eber had started dating but before they'd moved in together, on a dare from Eber Karl had tried putting a hand up Kelly's skirt while Eber ran into the supermarket for a new rack and a bottle of bubbly. "She digs you, man," Eber had been saying for some time then. "Even more than me. I swear it. She was all *about* you in high school, you were just too bent out of shape on that Kimberly chick to notice. I tell you what…thirty seconds alone together, you can get her off! Swear it, no lie. That chick comes like a man." But Kelly had given him such a confused, weary look of regret, sadness and dismay—said, "No, Karl. Just, no. Please. Did Eber put you up to that? Is that your-all's idea of a funny joke? We're adults now, Karl. Sheesh, you guys can grow up any time you feel like it…"—it had been weeks of self-imposed isolation, hating on himself, before he could face either one of them again. Thing was, he'd known it was wrong. Sure, she wore those short dresses, more like low-cut, super-sized T-shirts, and leather-thonged flip-flops, so she was all summer practically half-naked or making you think of her half-naked, and sure he liked it when she took out her hair clip and shook back her hair, the shiny, honeyed bump in her hair where the clip had been, more red than blonde. He'd felt until then, with her and Eber, that he was both invisible and boundlessly included, both at the same time—like he was not there at all, and like all the normal barriers between people must have been erased so he was not *Karl* any more, in the way he was *Karl* to other people. He was Eber's twin brother, and by the transitive property therefore Kelly's almost proxy-boyfriend. They could talk about everything together, the three of them—girls and drinking and bodily functions, stories about skanks and hos and favorite positions and how to get laid. Still, he'd known, in the seconds before he reached for her that it was just all wrong. But stupid or gullible or whatever you wanted to call him, he had to follow through, mainly because Eber had said so, but also because his hand was already going there—he had to see what it was like, what she acted like, what she did. And then she'd given him the look. Plucked his hand off, sighed, and said the thing about growing up. And a moment later, like she was trying to make it back up to him for having said it, "Another time and place, maybe, Karl. But not now, which as far as I can tell, means not *ever*. OK? You're a nice enough guy." There was a quaver in her voice that hadn't helped a bit. Had only caused him to long for her in a way he hadn't actually been longing for her when he first tried to grope her.

"I'm so sorry, Kelly."

"He put you up to it? What are you guys like automatically eighteen years old and retarded whenever you get in one another's company? You think it's *funny?*"

He shook his head. "I wouldn't say."

"Keep your hands to yourself, OK? Didn't your mother teach you?"

"Our mother's an asshole. She's been gone since forever. You know that, Kell. Didn't teach us nothing, nada, not a damn thing."

"Just…whatever. Chill. OK?"

And mostly, after he'd come back around to kicking it with them, it had been OK…only, it also *hadn't* been OK, and though she had for a while sometimes jokingly referred to *the time Karl tried to grab my ass*, he'd always pictured the thing between them, whatever it was, lying there, secretly having a life of its own and making everything else, as far as he was concerned, drift around its current, but invisibly and in such a way he couldn't always name or predict the outcome. Just, it was there. Quite possibly this was the main reason things were always failing for him, any time he found a new girl to like or date. He might have blamed it on Eber—*It's a known fact about twins, Hon, don't take it personal, it's just hard for us, harder than normal anyway, to form any other attachment*—but it wasn't Eber. It was always Kelly, possibly Kelly and Eber together, but mainly just Kelly.

Their second or third day back to the hospital, the first time they saw Eber up close in his hospital johnny, oxygen tube snaked under his nose, heart catheter, bruises up and down his arm, eyes rolled back under swollen lids, lips cracked and colorless, Karl had known two things simultaneously. One was that they no longer looked exactly alike, he and Eber. Eber was now easily ten years older in appearance. So here was a time-traveling vision of himself from the future, ten years out, maybe more, felled by some medical condition. The other was that Eber had never had a tattoo. Not a single one. Karl had known this of course, but had never fully absorbed it or somehow registered it: his brother did not have a single tattoo on him, anywhere. His legs, bare to the hips almost, spindly and inkless; arms bare and pale olive, covered in black arm hair, also inkless; and his shaved inkless chest that had been sawed open and stapled back shut with hideous blue Frankenstein clips— all of him was as tattoo-free as ancient relatives of theirs presumably buried in ditches in Romania. He'd never asked Eber specifically *why* or *why not* and hadn't really pushed him much about it. Once, flush from a little side deal he'd had harvesting gourmet mushrooms in the woods with a buddy of theirs—they looked to him more like dog turds than mushrooms and sold for almost as much as drugs, minus the risk—he'd offered to start Eber with a simple one color tattoo, whatever he wanted, a spade or a clover or whatever, but Eber had said no—*Not for me bro. No offense, I just don't need them or whatever it is like you do, don't need to make that kind of a statement, and besides I can't think of anything I'd actually want to have to see the rest of my life.* Karl never asked again. And now, seeing him in that hospital johnny, he understood something else—equally obvious—he felt certain he must have realized at least a time or two before: ink or no ink, he and Eber had never *actually* been the same person after all. Also, *not* knowing this, or not having believed it sufficiently, had always been the fuel, or the connecting wire to some of the fuel anyway, that made him want to go and get all the tattoos in the first place. He couldn't quite see how that worked yet, he just knew it was so. He knew it in his head from the voice that told him so, and in his body from the sudden reawakening of all his old cravings for a new tattoo. He even had a vision of what and where—some kind of funny spin on the old yin-yang symbol crossed with a single fish-tailed sperm cell, maybe on the small of his back or his left butt cheek.

"Hey, man," he'd said.

His brother's eyes rolled toward them and back up into his head and back to them again and he seemed almost to be smiling. "You all. You came. How do you like…my new zombie look?" There were pauses between the words, enough to make it difficult to get his meaning at first.

"Metal, man. You're one badass motherfucker."

"You should. See the other. Guy."

They didn't laugh exactly, but smiled and moved closer so whatever fucked up picture of them he was getting might come in a little more clearly. Some of the bruises on Eber's arm, Karl decided, almost looked like tattoos—one like a sheep, another like a distorted, multi-colored cloudburst.

Kelly said, "I hear they had to take him to the butcher shop. Finish the job. Couldn't put him back together."

Again there was the almost-smile and the eyes rolled away.

"You just relax, bro. They got you on the good stuff. You're going to have one fine tripped-out time for a while. OK, man?"

Eber's lips twitched. Nothing more.

In retrospect, he supposed it shouldn't have surprised anyone, least of all him. Waiting with her in hospital waiting rooms, they were misidentified as a couple by nursing staff often enough—*No, it's my brother. She's the common-law, whatever you want to call it. I'm the brother*—because everything about them must have suggested it, suggested couplehood, so often, in fact, it even began feeling like a foregone conclusion and mostly unacknowledged inevitability. Sometimes, if they were in a rush out the door or late getting one place to another and she couldn't find her keys or phone or a glove, she might slip and start calling him Eber. Then catching herself she'd swat him on the arm. *Quit confusing me! I know who's who.* But if she slipped and didn't catch herself and he pointed it out, she might get more riled and use a tone of voice that was harder to read, like she was aggrieved and joking and on the verge of other emotions he didn't have names for, all at the same time—*Karl, Eber, Eber, Karl! Whatever!* Some afternoons watching her asleep on his shoulder, he'd wonder what he was doing. *Why?* he'd think. And then, *Why not?* He didn't dare move or shift her head back against the chair cushion for fear of waking her—she slept so poorly even in the best of times. Painful minutes on end while his arm fell asleep all the way to his fingertips and the crick in his neck from sitting like this to keep her from slipping became almost too much to bear, he'd wait it out and watch her sleep, convinced she was the most desirable woman on the planet and also the one woman with whom he most positively should never ever hook up.

He slept on the couch in her and Eber's living room, or in the easy chair at his own place, if that's where they ended up crashing, both of them continually on call for Eber, eating take-out and fast food together, spelling each other and calling in sick at work, carpooling because her Mustang was still out of commission and now was not the time to get it to the shop. It wasn't grief, finally, to catalyze things. More it was a feeling that they'd come to the end of an unbearable and confining pretense. Released to each other in some new private hell—really a glowing ring of sentiment, theirs alone, and which wasn't necessarily all bad, though it was sure enough permeated with feelings of pain and grief and loss and guilt—it had seemed to him the only and most obvious, inevitable thing to do: to hold her, bare himself, all one hundred ninety-five inked pounds of himself, and make love to her.

They'd had some wine with their dinner, and watching her walk away with plates, carrying them balanced on her wrist to the sink in her kitchen, the tilt of her hips, her bare feet, belt undone because she'd been sitting cross-legged on the floor and she always did that when she was sitting like that, it occurred to him how fully and completely alone and available to each other they were. Anything at all could happen now, anything *should* happen, no one had to know. Eber's condition had more or less plateaued; still, no one could say what kind of recovery he'd make. Days and days of this remained. They were in the long, slow homestretch toward an indeterminate end. What the hell. "Leave those, Hon. It's my turn," he said. And then quickly, because he knew such moments were as fleeting as they were potentially indelible and so you needed to act at once, grab on, take some solid form of action, or forget it, he'd slipped up behind her there at the sink and enfolded her in his arms. Lowered his face to her neck and breathed fully the smell of her that had been driving him so crazy all week, and felt her sink back against him. The water was still running.

"Karl," she said. "Are you sure?"

He said nothing right away. Held her and waited. "Hell no. Yeah. I think so. Why? What about you?"

"I don't know."

"Yeah."

But she didn't move or attempt to move and moments later, hands sliding over her, under her shirt, between her legs, he remembered Eber's dare to him, his words to describe it—*comes like a man, thirty seconds, I swear it*—and as quickly forced the thought back. Pictured himself and Eber as matching miniature fighter-figures on a huge, empty field, and then as she turned towards him in his arms, opening herself, he made the figures go away—made them smaller and smaller until they weren't there. Forced back all thoughts of Eber, and as much as he was able to, did not register anything according to Eber or Eber's tone or Eber's way of seeing the rest of that night and the nights to follow that were his and Kelly's alone.

On it went until the morning, mid-December, just a few days short of Eber's official release from Sacred Heart, when they showed half an hour earlier than usual, and stepping from the elevator hand-in-hand into the long term care wing, there was Eber—I.V. tree in hand, pushing his way along the corridor to them. "You two," he said then, grinning wide enough and shaking his head so that at first Karl thought it might all turn out OK. Might not be the big deal blowout after all—might be something they'd laugh about later. Might even be a simple easy trade-off. *You want Kelly? You two want that? Hey man, my blessings.* But the smile was Eber's way of suckering them close enough to be sure, and then to speak his mind. Karl didn't look at Kelly to see how she was taking any of this, but felt the place where his hand stayed fused with hers like a heart, a fucked-up heart with no feeling, pumping along poison. "I shoulda known. You fucks. Shoulda fucking died, huh. That would've made things a little easier, huh? So sorry, bro. Didn't quite work out like that, did it. But hey… gain a ho, lose a bro."

Watching Eber drift away from them back up the corridor in his hospital slippers, Karl had felt certain he should do something solid now—go after him, yell, plead, anything to undo the damage— and equally certain that he should not. He should let Eber cool off on his own. Let him make his feeble, old-man way alone back to his lame hospital bed, and lie there thinking. They could come back tomorrow or the day after to see what was what.

"Don't," he said, when he sensed Kelly about to start after Eber. "Don't. Just…let's get out of here. You've got, what, like an hour before you need to be to work?" Until about a year ago when the chemicals finally got to her, she'd done hair at one of the better places downtown. Now she set appointments, answered phones and did some light bookkeeping for an acupuncturist's office on the north side called *Points of Return*.

And again on the elevator ride down, seeing their smudged reflections in the banged up sheet metal paneling of the interior, and in the visitor parking lot, watching her slide across the bench seat of his truck to be nearer to him, he'd had the feeling culminating actions or words were required, but he couldn't think of what they should be. Not another animal. Not a tattoo or a drink. What? The pig, he remembered, looking over the menagerie, had actually come from their father in happier childhood times, and the joke about it was that it had a peg leg. *Because*, as their dad had told them, *a pig that good you want to keep him around...you don't want to just kill him.* Eber had re-discovered it in a box of clutter and miscellaneous junk in the back of a closet that past summer, more tan than pink by then, and they'd glued it to the dashboard after a midnight naked swim to the raft and back at the big resort in Idaho. But stupidly, because of the dark or because they'd forgotten which side the pig's peg leg was on, they'd glued it in wrong-side out so a passenger who didn't know to look for it wouldn't see the peg leg or get the joke. "Kell," he said, thinking he should at least say something about what had happened, maybe suggest a plan for returning tomorrow, when he noticed the flush creeping up her neck and that irresistible look on her face that combined longing and surrender, and he knew all she wanted for now was to forget. *Forget, forget,* said the voice in his head. "Never mind," he said, and pointed the truck back down the hill to her place.

The next day Eber was gone. Checked himself out and left billing and insurance information for himself at their mother's in California, though they hadn't seen her in going on thirty years, and aside from annual birthday and Christmas cards, always perfectly timed, always with matching, freshly minted 50-dollar bills in them and the same inscription—*Happiest holiday wishes!* or *Birthday wishes! Love, Your Mom*—and the occasional phone call, they had had nothing to do with her. At first Karl thought it must be some kind of ridiculous joke. Eber would never go there. Not in a million years. Where had he even gotten a phone number for her? Four-five voicemail messages later he gave up. *Dude, look it's me again. Man, look, it's totally over between me and Kelly, whatever it was. OK? It was never anything to start with. What the fuck. So you can just come on home now. California's not your scene, man! Bunch of surfer fags and skanks. Come on. What the fuck?...Dude, look, it's me again. I can't keep doing this, but look, man, I'm really sorry. I don't know how many different ways I can say it, if you're even getting the messages. But whatever. I'm fucking sorry, man, and whatever you want from me, anything at all. Name your price. You know that's always been the case. I love you, man, but you can't just up and vanish on us...I mean...you can't just do this shit, OK? It ain't right! Ain't according to the plan...Hey, man, it's me again...* The last time he tried calling he got an automatic disconnect message. He knew better than to try any more. In no time the cell phone company would recycle Eber's number and he'd be blabbering to some stranger about the hole Eber had blown in his heart when he'd left town, the pointlessness of it all, the empty days marching along one after another, same shirt, same shoes, same job, same shit different day. Sunrise, sunset. Every day the same without Eber. He no longer had the first idea where Eber was, any of his thoughts or feelings or what he might be doing with his time. Didn't get a signal on any of it. Even the day after he'd gotten the new tattoo and had to avoid sitting, had to drive tilted up awkwardly on one butt cheek because it hurt so much otherwise—nothing. Maybe it's the timer-thing in his heart, he thought. Maybe with the new electrical device, time-keeper or whatever, implanted there to keep things steady, some essential connection between himself and Eber had been cut. If there was a new, steadier mechanical stutter in his own heart to echo Eber's, he didn't feel it.

As with all emblematic-seeming, marker-like objects (and life in general, really), Karl knew there was a hidden meaning or pattern only if you chose to see it and to think so, and choosing or not choosing to think so was not necessarily weird or demented or stupid, wasn't even right or wrong. It was just another decision you had to make, like so many other things—what hat to wear, or whether to use the freeway to get to work or take the frontage roads. Didn't ultimately matter or mean anything. So, on the one hand he was perfectly aware that all he was witnessing was a simple matter of the physical limitations of Gorilla Super Glue drunkenly misapplied to a dirty surface finally giving up its bond after months and temperature fluctuations that could destroy brick and mortar. Eventually one of the animals was going to pop off. It had to happen. On the other hand, it had been long enough that if he chose to read the failing glue as a sign or signal, call to action, he could do that. He was in his rights.

The one to go first was the one they'd glued in last—the eagle. He wished he remembered anything specific about what it had been stuck there to commemorate. That night they'd been at the bicycle trailhead by the military graveyard, hot-boxing a joint of Eber's excellent hydroponic medical *purple haze* and watching the sunset. In the midst of it, Karl had remembered the eagle and extracted it from his pants pocket to show Eber. "Oh, hey," he'd said, "look—ain't exactly a Caracara, but looks kind of like one anyway," and held it up for both of them to admire in the glorious sunset light, as he narrated for Eber some of the details about the kid at the pawn shop he'd bought it off of. Later, they'd walked on the trail and had a howlingly fun time, lost in the ravine by the river after the sun vanished and before the moon rose. Somewhere in there they'd gotten soaked to the knees and he must have given the eagle to Eber. Then Karl had dropped Eber back at his and Kelly's apartment, said, "Buenos noches, motherfucker," ate take-out at Arby's and went home to crash instantly and dreamlessly on the easy chair in front of the TV. Next morning, seeing the eagle there on his dashboard, he'd wondered about it and for a while tried to recollect what it commemorated— the specifics of what they'd done and what the eagle might stand for. But then there'd been the early cold snap and Eber had had his heart attack, after which Karl never gave it much thought again.

The weather had been strange all week, and was strangest the day the eagle fell off—gusts of backward-blowing torrential spring rain and intermittent sunshine, thunder, rainbows, crazy pockets of air so hot and humid it felt like some tropical front blown straight from California to the interior of Washington state, then the sheets of icy rain. He half-expected pineapple groves to materialize, and lost macaws, bewildered and half-frozen to death by the sudden transport. Later, hail the size of dimes coated the streets in slushy globules, banishing all fanciful tropical visions, and he splashed his way home through streaky sun rocking to the familiar tones of one of Eber's old mixes—favorite stuff from the early 90's, when music was still music and still good. Stuff he hadn't heard in eons but which felt as pleasing as ever vibrating the speaker cone by his left leg and causing the same happy fluctuations in his inner ear and coursing through all of his synapses. What the hell. Where was Eber, anyway? He should just come on home already. Only when he rolled to a stop at the end of his duplex driveway did he notice: the eagle was gone. Impossible. Who would have stolen it? Took him a few minutes groping along the floor of the truck cab in the dwindling light to find it—feet and tail feathers still coated in dirty, cracked, and yellowy Gorilla Super Glue—and another few minutes to realize that in fact all the animals were now getting a little wobbly in their footing. The cow in particular felt almost ready to go and could be rocked up slightly on her hind legs. Not quite there. Close. Sure, he thought. Of course. *Time.* Time passes, things change. Whatever you were so worried about didn't actually matter that much.

And without thinking it through any further he turned, shoulder checked, and backed out of the driveway, headed for Kelly's.

Their last night together she'd told him something he hadn't quite been able to believe or digest and had consequently put out of his mind altogether. This was in January, not long after Eber's disappearance, during the period in which their habit of spending days and nights together along with the general confusion and loss surrounding Eber's absence kept them regularly hanging out—eating together, sleeping together, brushing and flossing, getting steadily so caught up in a pattern it was almost hard to believe there'd been a time they weren't this way. He couldn't say who was comforting whom, or if there even was anything like *comforting* going on between them. Many of Eber's shirts became his own again—favorite old snap shirts he'd forgotten he'd ever loaned or forfeited to Eber, and 501s he felt sure he must have handed off at one time or another. Even a pair of felt-lined Sorels he'd recently coveted and Eber's favorite bad-ass cowboy boots finished in flaking sea-bass. Some days, slumping beside Kelly in the couch cushions shaped exactly to

Eber, hand on her hip or leg, flipping through the channels, taking in all their old favorite shows, he wondered who he even was anymore. If somewhere along the line he hadn't maybe passively subsumed some or all of Eber to become a new covalent conglomerate of the two brothers together—the new and improved Karleber. Or maybe Eberkarl. Whatever. It didn't feel wrong exactly, but it also definitely didn't feel right.

The night he finally mentioned something about it to Kelly, she gave him the look again—the same one she'd begun with that first night, when he tried groping her, only this time mixed with the knowing tenderness and impatience that can only occur between people who've been sleeping together a long time. "Feeling guilty?"

He shook his head.

"Don't you know this already, Karl?"

"Know what?"

"Let's put it to you like this." She raked fingers through her hair and waited long enough, staring him down that he had time to reconsider what the look might actually mean and to forget some of what they were talking about. Maybe the look was something else altogether, like conjuring spirits—seeing through him to conjure ancestral, predestined aspects of his personality no one else even knew about. Maybe in her time at *Points of Return*, seeing people stuck with pins and prescribed ancient herbal remedies, something had rubbed off on her, giving her new mystical powers to see past, present and future. "Why do you think you got all those tattoos?"

"Tattoos?" He'd shrugged. "I don't know. I like them?"

"Try again."

"They're all different, I guess. So, different reasons each time. You know. This one, I…"

"No, Karl. No. It's like a fence, isn't it. Like a little fence you built up around yourself. So now you've got Eber's girlfriend and his apartment, pretty much, if you want it, everything that was his, his clothes and couch and whatever else, it's all yours, and so you're sitting around here wondering what the hell. How did it happen that you're turning into this guy who isn't even himself anymore? But it's because you're looking at everything *backwards*. Right? Whatever it was you were trying to keep in and hold back with those tattoos—" she snapped her fingers "—poof. It's gone. See? Because Eber's gone." She snapped her fingers again. "Poof, like that. You got all the stuff, so now there's no more fence, no more Eber, you don't have to worry anymore, so the question now is *what are you going to do* because it's clear you're guilty as fuck."

"That's crazy talk. There's no *fence*." He laughed and swigged from his beer. Drained it and set it noisily on the floor.

"That's what I said. Exactly what I said. No fence."

"No! For fuck's sake. I mean there never was any fucking *fence*, girl. Jeez. That's crazy talk." And pushing up from the couch cushions he'd known, from the pitch of his own voice and the familiar prickle through his scalp that he needed to get out of here and fast, because he was on the verge of some kind of wall-punching violence or other stupidity he'd only regret.

"You gotta go, Karl," Kelly said. She'd stood too and something new in her stance and bearing reminded him of the fact that once, years earlier, she'd earned an advanced belt in one form of martial arts or another. Not Karate. One of the others. More likely than not if he tried anything funny or violent he'd just end up flipped on his back or in some kind of finger-breaking death grip. Fuck that shit.

"Don't I know it."

"You call when you get things sorted, Karl."

"No, *you* call."

She shook her head. "That's not how it works, Hon, and you know that. I can't say I'll be waiting, but I will be...for a while anyway. You know, I..." she said, and shook her head some more. "Never mind."

"What."

"You can always try."

"Fuck you, *try*. Jesus."

"You're stuck, Hon. Come on. We both are. It's time to just kind of…let go."

"*You're* stuck."

"That's what I just said, Karl. Now leave."

That was the end of it. Weeks now, months—three, to be exact—there hadn't been a word between them. He'd even stopped driving by her place to see if she was there still or if anyone was keeping her company, and it occurred to him now as he threaded his way down the familiar side streets and hills to her place—one of a handful of Victorian silver-miner's mansions carved up into apartments and stranded between crack houses with boarded shut windows and yuppie reno-projects in the "artsy" part of town—that it might already be too late. Way too late. Might be she'd flown town, summoned by Eber, or just moved on of her own accord. It happened all the time. No. She was a hometown girl. Lived here all her life, probably never leave. Beyond that though, there was no saying. She was as fine-looking a woman as he'd ever known or laid eyes on, and easy to be around. It'd be surprising in the extreme if she stayed single for long.

As if reflective of his darkening prospects the sky lowered, black as fumes, and raindrops the size of lemons pelted his windshield. Wind swung trees around wildly on their roots, showering shattered twigs and pine cones down on him. For a time he had to sit curbside, waiting it out, watching the world turn upside down from wind and rain, brightening and dimming again with each lightning flash, so that by the time he was finally able to step out and make a run for it, splashing his way across the slushy, muddy yard to the front door of her building, he felt almost stoned from all the strobing, barometric commotion and ozone-laced oxygen. He was pretty sure he knew exactly how things would happen from here. Saw himself mounting the stairs super-fast, two and three at a time, and standing in the darkened hall outside her door, knocking once to be let in and then, remembering, fishing the copy of her key from inside his pocket, turning it, and entering. The kitchen where he'd first embraced her would be the same still, her dishes stacked and lined up on the drain board, coffeemaker in its spot by the stove, white mugs on top. Same creaky boards under foot as he made his way down the hall past the living room where Eber had collapsed—the hippy-print bedspread on the wall beside the couch to cover the water stains there making him think of camels and hashish and camping in the desert, causing him always to smell patchouli incense whether or not any was burning. The hand-knit afghan from her grandmother draped over the back cushions, and braided rag rug where Eber had lain and where the medics had evidently zapped him back to life all those months ago. Same drafty window leaking cold outside air in currents through the overheated room. All of it the same. Down the hall he'd go, to her bedroom—door slightly ajar—push it open without knocking, and then he'd rush in on them. The man inside, whoever it was with Kelly—Eber, *not*-Eber—might see him entering, might not. "Surprise, motherfucker!" Karl would yell and then lift and crush, crush, crush the man into a death-dealing bear hug until ribs, arms, shoulders, chest, all bones popped and went slack, and then the man would just disappear back to wherever he'd come from and he'd have Kelly to himself again. "See?" he'd say then. "See? " He didn't know what he'd say beyond that or what exactly he'd want to cause her to see about himself.

Or...not. Maybe he'd hang there in the doorway awhile watching, voyeur-style, appreciating the scene, the sexiness—shadow-double of himself alongside Kelly or hunched up over her, making love to her, making her come. He'd whisper his personal goodbyes and turn and head back down the hall and outside again to his truck, surrendered to a lifetime alone, no Kelly, no Eber. Maybe he'd watch awhile first to see if it was always true, what Eber had said—*thirty seconds. I swear it!*—true with all men that is, or only them? Was it all the same, whomever she made love to? He supposed it was. He supposed it was not.

Meanwhile, here he was in the window reflections of the living room and in the blotchy antique mirror above the hearth—downward sloping to allow a wide-angle god's-eye view of the living room and the floor where Eber had fallen—distorted and warped by time or heat, worn to its black backing in chunks and patches so that depending where he stood, and how, he could cause pieces of himself to vanish, a shard of head, half an arm, portions of his face erased while other pieces floated out of place, flattened or elongated, engulfed in darkness. Karl the tattooed man. Karl, the freak twin with all the ink. Karl, the shadow man who just always wanted to be a little more than Eber's twin, a little more than Eber. *Yeah*, he mouthed. *Well, fuck that. Fuck you, Eber. Just, fuck you.* He watched the pieces shift and go out of focus and realign again, fascinated by something he couldn't name or put a finger on in all the distortion—some essential *un*likeness to himself and Eber he'd never fully understood and which he had no name for...so fascinated he almost missed her coming up behind him from the shadows, baseball bat in hand. Same old T-shirt dress and bare feet, same cleft chin and weary calm, same woman they'd both loved. "Hey," he said, and turned to her, arms open—"It's me!"—all the pieces sliding away again in his peripheral vision so fast he was almost able to glimpse, in the seconds before they disintegrated and she leaned up her shoulders readying for the swing, the perfect understanding of who he was and what he'd always been.

HALF AS HAPPY

SUMMER AFTERNOONS Stan would come home from his work at the mortgage lending office in town, ten minutes away, for lunch. He'd sit by the pool sipping a cold Kokanee with his usual sandwich of turkey and ham on a whole-grain bun or organic six-grain bread, with mustard and no mayo, watching Heidi swim. There was less and less of her to watch, less even than in May when school let out. The bones in her ankles and feet had begun showing again and there was that pleasing, flaring, egg-shaped concavity about each of her collarbones and indented around her hips, as well—things he had loved about her years ago, before they were even married, and which he had forgotten because of how long they'd lain hidden under new layers of her flesh, flesh he'd loved, as well, though differently. She swam regardless of any weather, and also, regardless of weather, now that she was on the diet, walked her seven-eight miles through the woods surrounding their property, following rail beds and dusty roads of gravel and sand. He watched her flit through the pale green water of their pool, one hand extended for the far wall and her eyelids lowered, and at 12:45 when his sandwich was gone and more than half of his Kokanee, he rose and went to stand at the side of the pool with a towel held open for her. He knew this was when she'd wish him to stop her. He waited for the sound of her interrupted kicks and the water splashing up as she emerged out of it, water sliding from her back and arms as she hoisted herself up, and then he stood aside admiring her, bare in the noon light.

Sometimes, at this point, they'd exchange greetings and other words having to do with their respective mornings. Mostly, he said nothing. He held the towel and then watched her rub it around her shoulders and against the back of her head, then knot it between her breasts and tilt her head to the side to wring water from her hair or pound water from inside one of her ears. He returned to his chair and the remainder of his beer sweating onto the stone, tilted back with his face in the sun and his eyes shut, listening.

They had been married eighteen years and known each other four more years than that in college. Because of this, he knew, almost before she said it, most of what she was going to tell him, though not always the words she'd choose or the final outcome of the thing she was saying. The utterances, the words chosen, went adrift like whatever was stuck floating on the top or the bottom of the pool—needles and twigs and leaves, dead bugs, the film of a day's dust—leaving him with the impression that he was the water in communion with her, containing and embracing her, or she was the water surrounding him and he had hardly to think or to turn or to move in order to understand and be understood. Sometimes they didn't speak at all, and still he felt, in the silence, that he was understanding her.

Next came the sound of her flip-flops on the hot slate slabs surrounding the pool and the creak of her chair (less and less of a creak, now she was so much thinner again) accepting her weight, the light musical crackle of her clearing her throat, and then silence. Pages turning as she read. Birds. More throat clearing. A word. Two words. Sometimes he slept.

WHEN FRIENDS OF HERS visited from out of town (all of her best friends lived far away and came in the summer), or when members of his own family descended on them with wives and children (his closest relatives were male, two brothers and a cousin, all three with blond, child-bearing wives and too many children in various stages of growth to keep up on), or when work friends came around, he showed them first to the pool. Or, if not first, very soon after they'd arrived. If they were new guests he instructed them on how to reel and unreel the sheet of bubbled plastic covering the water between swims; with one bare toe he held down the button controlling the winding mechanism and watched their faces as the sheet drew back from the water, no sound but the hum of machinery and water rippling over itself. Murky green, on fire from the sunset at evening or flashing pieces of the afternoon sun, or, at night lit by underwater lamps. Jade made liquid. He stood by and waited for their responses—always the same, more or less, with variations—the awestruck smiles and looks of longing as it dawned on them that, yes, here was what they wanted and needed, had wanted all day, in fact. To swim! Strip, plunge, purge, be clean, free of the heat and dust, changed back to their original, private, water-weighted selves! "Swim as late as you want," he'd hear himself saying as soon as the cover was wound fully back. "You can wear a suit, if you like, or go like Heidi and me, au naturale. As you can see, no neighbors to speak of, unless you count the deer. The occasional eagle or blue heron." He didn't know why he always said this part about the skinny-dipping; they rarely took him up on it and he hated the sound of his voice saying it. Though he longed for flashes of bare flesh other than his wife's flitting in and out of sight through that water, he was seldom so rewarded. Seldom, but not never.

Once, late at a meeting of other regional branch managers, he'd come home closer to three for his lunch to find Heidi with her oldest girlhood friend, a woman named Siam, naked and sprawled on the slate by the water, both on their backs, sharing a single towel and reading from a single paperback novel, and laughing. This was early in the summer she began dissolving through water, a few weeks after the close of classes and less time than that since putting aside the last of her administrative duties as Associate Dean for the college. He was so struck by the sight of it, their half-entwined limbs, wrists nearly indistinguishable one from the other, each one's loveliness multiplied by the other's—that is, its loveliness made more ineffable by its likeness in shape and color to the other—that he did not understand at first what was happening. Did not necessarily identify either woman as Heidi until after several moments of having stood there in the shade of the yew tree by the carport, beer in hand, immobilized by the overwhelming lushness of it all and feeling gradually, giddily, more and more pissed off. That was *his* pool, *his* wife, and…(their laughter went on unchecked, neither woman aware of his presence) *his book* they were reading from and laughing at! A new Tom Clancy he'd started just last week, or the week before, and had not gotten more than 50 pages into. He did not creep stealthily up on them to confirm his worst suspicions or to witness the innocent convergence of their flesh (he knew it was innocent, though knowing did nothing to allay his consternation or jealousy). He turned and went back the way he'd come. Sat in the sunken living room, the one he'd decorated with elk and zebra skins, on his old leather couch beside the glassed shelves of elephant relics from around the world—figurines, bones, plaques, masks, and carved tusks. He ate his sandwich and listened to their voices and wondered at the transformation his imagination had wrought: these were the same voices he'd heard on entering the house only moments ago, and which had drawn him happily outside, beer and sandwich in hand, ready to join the fun. And he was struck at his powerlessness to change that transformation though it all had occurred in *his* head from start to finish, the whole shooting match, and was no one else's business but his own. Probably.

The trouble with Heidi: she was not nearly as easy to know as people always seemed to assume on a first impression, and she didn't actually want half of what she seemed most actively to crave or seek out. He thought he might be the only one to really know this about her, and though he was fairly certain it bore some relationship to her past (it was as unlike his as imaginable, the jumble of Air Force bases she'd grown up on across the continent and elsewhere, and the seemingly endless array of instant, temporary friendships spiked into intimacy by the suddenness of arrival and inevitability of leaving), he was not always clear what that relationship was. She preferred strangers. She preferred fleeting contact with fascinating people, and would be "positively in love," she said sometimes, with a man or woman she'd met only hours earlier. Of course, there were exceptions: him, Siam, her father, a few others. But mostly she "loved" people she couldn't really know. She seemed, to him even, at times, to love the obstacles to knowing them as much as she loved *them*—the distance and expense of travel and the barely missed opportunities for having taken up parallel or convergent roads at some former point in life. *Oh, if only…if I'd only known you then!* Always the same lament.

But this was different. This was Siam who'd also known Heidi since forever and whose affection might as easily exclude him, and who, he had to admit it, he'd always found sort of sexy—because of her closeness to Heidi, sure, and also because she was just a damn fine woman to look at, fresh and pretty, with thick black eyelashes and eyebrows, and always saying the first thing that came to her mind. Yes, he could understand why Heidi would want her.

He picked crumbs from his plate, crinkled his beer can, wiped his mouth, and waited until Heidi showed at the sliding glass door. She was no longer naked but wound up in some kind of toga or terrycloth beach wrap he didn't recognize, sudden, backlit, and unable to conceal a look of unguarded pleasure as he was unable, for the moment, to conceal his jealousy and aggravation. "Well, look…" she said. "What are you doing in the dark, Stan? Why didn't you come out and tell us you were home? We were waiting all this time. I thought I heard…" He couldn't tell her words apart exactly or attach them to their meanings. Something was wrong. Something had gone wrong in his head to prevent him from really taking her in. He was too mad and confused—mainly mad at himself—and the buzz of his pulse was almost enough to drown her out.

"Did I have to?" he said. The words stuck against his palette, vibrating. "Had a few things to think over."

"Everything OK? Something at work?"

He didn't answer right away. "Always something wrong at work, honey. You know that."

Nothing more came of it, or not much, anyway. He returned, that night, to a late dinner of broiled trout, fresh ears of corn (she didn't touch it), and salad and beans from the garden. They all three sat outside on deck chairs until the mosquitoes were too much to bear, and by the time the food was gone, and the wine, he could almost imagine he'd managed once again to free himself of the feelings that had caught him off guard earlier that afternoon. The little gestures between the two women now seemed so much the same as ever, he could hardly understand how that was also him, hunched in the living room and brooding, or stuck by the yew tree. He was himself again, easy and confident, full of his usual stories: the tale of six martinis; the time his brother ate a golf ball; Wencel, the new, young re-fi guy who didn't shave, exactly, but left a neat quarter-inch of growth around his jaws. "Cultivated sloth," he said icily. "Tell me, what's it about, Siam? You're a single girl—you should know." And inside the conversation had gone on as well—a new bottle of wine, each woman on a floor pillow, him behind them on the couch. Like old times.

Hours later, jolted out of his sleep by a noise or sudden spike in his metabolism related to the wine, he lay awake and remembered: the two women on the towel, their pale bronze arms and shoulders together and the sound of their voices and laughter. It was all so pretty and exclusive, it had to have some corollary in the flesh, didn't it, imagined if not acted upon? How else did it exist in his mind, why else did he perceive it? Closer now, he saw them again—their skin imprinted with the weave of their shared towel, sweat trapped and beaded under hair and in the creased stubble of their armpits, sweat beading on the bridge of Heidi's nose as it always did. All of it perfectly real. Of course. How else could it have been?

He rolled to her and slung an arm over her hip. But if he woke her now she would receive him too warmly, confusing everything.

He knew it. She'd lean her hips to his, speak out of her dreams and open her body, just like that. Why? Wasn't there some duplicity in it? Wouldn't she all the more ardently embrace him to fake him out and keep him off track, put him back to sleep—or, worse yet, use him as the stand-in for whatever she truly desired?

A glass of milk, he thought, and slipped from bed. Hot milk and two aspirin.

It was no use. All night he wandered the house bare-footed, draped in a dusty, skin-scratching blanket from the leather couch, his dead grandmother's. That night and most of the night after, until Siam had gone. He lay in the sunken living room thinking about her and then he got up again. He looked out at the pool in the moonlight, and he wondered what he wanted and why, and how to get shut of it all, how to turn it around in his mind again so it meant something, but he never found any answers he liked. "Siam, Siam," he muttered, as if it were a curse. He watched *Rear Window* a number of times in bits and pieces, rewinding to his favorite scenes and wandering off again—the ones with Jimmy Stewart cranky and reluctant at the hands of his interfering fiancée (it was pure genius, he thought—more ingenious than any of the hokey spying or strangled pets or body parts in the flowerbed detective nonsense that made up the rest of the film—pretending anyone in his right mind would feel a moment's resentment or hesitation giving up bachelorhood for Grace Kelly. Pure fantasy, but so pleasing!). Grace, he thought, in those scenes, was a little like Heidi at her best—sweet, hurt, dissembling, nervy—and though he was no adventuring photographer, he knew he at least *looked* a little like the convalescing Jimmy Stewart—lanky and dark-haired, and with the same quirks of personality, the same meddlesome, well-meaning, but hobbled crankiness.

He was glad when Siam left, though he did not say so. He said, "Ah, Siam of the earnest smile," and waited for Heidi's response, but she was busy with what she was reading. He said, "Bet you two will miss each other a bunch, huh. How long was it this time?" Again, nothing. Birds sang. Something splashed in and out of the pool—an overgrown insect or small bird. He loosened his tie and tilted his head back, exhausted. "She'll be back," he said. "I'm sure." "I'm sure." Her voice came so quickly after his he was not sure which of them had spoken first or if either of them had said anything at all. Again he slept.

HE COULDN'T DENY, at first, that the less of her there was to look at, the more complete was his pleasure in looking. Mostly. He saw the irony in this, and liked the puzzle it presented. At times he thought maybe she was responding to some need in his eye—intuitively melting herself back to the proportions of female attractiveness she'd once embodied to him so effortlessly; shedding herself in order to show him again the spoon-like bend of her shins, the arched and bony feet. But if that were the case, she'd been perfect sometime back in June, more perfect than that by mid-July, and less and less so as time went on. He wondered if she was intending, ultimately, to starve herself out of existence, and, if so, if she might briefly transform to a single, radiant, indented surface of inscrutable beauty just before vanishing, a shell or bone, or if she'd begin moderating the diet at some point and padding herself up again; he wondered if he should trust her, or if he'd know when he ought, reasonably speaking, to step in and save her, or bring it up at all. There was a new insular solemnity about her, since Siam's visit, and at times he'd catch himself watching her with a kind of disgust and bewildered impatience he didn't recognize, wondering, what would come into view next? What would be left in another few weeks or months? "Enough," he wanted to say. "Enough is enough."

They made love as often as they ever had—once or twice a week, sometimes more, sometimes at night, sometimes on his lunch hour. If it was during his lunch hour there was generally a ritual for it. Stan did not undress. Not completely. His tie stayed knotted, cufflinks clipped on, wingtips tied, socks up, gold watch fastened—as if part of him were still at work. Always there was the clatter of keys and change in his pockets as his pants and boxers fell around his ankles to the slate, just before he entered her. Afterward, he'd kneel gingerly by the pool, rinsing his hands and face. He'd stand back shaking away water and grinning lopsidedly at her. "*That's* what I call a lunch break," he might say, or, "Sure as fuck beats two vodka martinis and a cheeseburger with Castille at The Steam Plant!" or, "Better than a protein pack and two scoops of fiber any day, huh?"

Early the morning of her departure Siam had said that she couldn't understand how they did it—how he and Heidi hung in through all these years together and stayed so impossibly happy. The two of them were alone, in the kitchen, sharing a quick breakfast and speaking in hushed tones, not to wake Heidi. "Happy?" he'd asked. "What makes you say so?" and regretted the words instantly. "*Of course*," he should have said sarcastically, like the Jimmy Stewart character: "*Why thank you, as happy as can be.*"

"Oh, come on, it's all over the place," she'd said. She broke off a bit of scone and put it on her tongue. Her lower teeth, he noticed, were pointy and too crowded together in the front, and her tongue had an oddly pointed shape as well. He watched her chewing, her jaw moving side-to-side, and thought how strange to be sharing this intimate hour of dawn with her, alone, after not sleeping. Almost like they were new lovers. "The house," she went on, "the food, the elephant safari stuff, the pool, the way…just everything. The way you fit. How supportive you are in whatever she does and you don't tie her down. I mean, I admire that so much in you guys."

He shrugged. Sipped his coffee. "A marriage is always a work in progress. No telling how it'll go. We were just a couple of maladjusted misfits when we met and we're still a couple of maladjusted misfits…"

"If I'm ever half as happy," she whipped her hair to one side and leaned over her plate, biting off another chunk of scone, "if I do half as well as you two together, I'll consider myself lucky."

"Lucky. I guess you could call it that." He shrugged. "Two people meet, they fall in love, boom. That's all she wrote. The rest is work."

He knew her story—the three marriages gone bad, the men who came and went, the two abortions. They were oldest girlfriends, she and Heidi. Soul-mates. Her teeth were pointy and too crowded and her tongue was orange. She was an inch shorter than Heidi, maybe ten pounds heavier now, and darker complected, and two days ago, coming home to find them naked alone in the sun he'd been surprised at the amount of body-hair on her; surprised, too, at how alike the two women were—their stomachs the same length and shape, breasts turning out the same way, one set of nipples darker, the other more pink, arms and shoulders matched.

She lifted his coffee cup and sipped from it, replacing it again in front of him, blinking. "I'm jealous," she said.

"*I'm* jealous. You've known her how many years longer than I have?"

She waved him off. "Talk about your maladjusted misfits."

On the drive to the airport where he'd drop her before continuing on to work, this conversation didn't resume. The exhaust on his fifteen year-old Jeep was shot and too loud to talk over, especially with the windows down to cut the fumes. He knew how incongruous this must seem to her and felt pleased with himself—in a mood, suddenly, to take stock of everything in his life: clean-cut, forty-two year-old hipster in a banker's suit, home-owning and long married, en route to the mortgage lending office he managed, oil-burning Jeep he could afford to fix (hell, to buy outright) six times over but probably never would unless he felt like it, Siam beside him, former flower child, pretty in a pseudo-Indian shawl and some kind of expensive black pumps, freshly made up and set to fly business-class back to Denver. Hot! *Look at us*, he wanted to say, recognizing his vanity and reveling in it, simultaneously—really having a good time. He worked the clutch and rattled over the bumps, down the dusty dirt road to the paved county road and out to the highway. He wanted to point out everything he saw for her—the light along the edges of the trees, the sweet burnt-fruit smell of pine and drying grasses, the railroad trestle at the bottom of their hill, the arched stone underpass, and the sign at the intersection shot through with buckshot by his crazy neighbor (gone now), rusted bullet holes pocking the letters, rendering them misaligned and three-dimensional: NOT A THROUGH ROAD. And at perfectly timed intervals (perhaps to disarm him, he couldn't say) when their eyes had not met for a few moments and there was no way to read it, she'd reach across the seat for the sip-cup of coffee between his legs, lift and drink from it and lower it again between his legs. She gazed evenly out the window or straight ahead at the dash between swallows. Again her hand appeared in his lap and again vanished, returning the cup—her nails neatly trimmed and fingers tan—again the sip-cup rested warmly in his crotch. He remembered Heidi at the front door in her summer bathrobe, hair mashed on one side from sleep, hugging Siam and saying, "Goodbye, goodbye—I love you, Sammy. Goodbye." They were so alike, with their hair falling over each other's arms, and arms around each other's shoulders, if he narrowed his eyes slightly, allowing things to blur, it was not like seeing two people embrace but more like watching a single entity of matched parts and terrible beauty in the process of dividing itself in two. Outside, the Jeep had stood, idling. "Goodbye, goodbye," they called through the open door.

"You take care of yourself," he told her at the airport. He lifted her bags from the back seat but did not move to embrace her. He knew how that might turn out, his hands wandering over her waist and guiding her against him, fingers pressing into all that luxuriant thickness of muscle and flesh, her whispering into his neck before detaching herself: *Come see me in Denver.* Oh, she wanted him all right. That was plain. And he... He shoved his hands into his pockets and leaned toward her, mock-grinning, Jimmy Stewart again. "You be sure and come again sometime, real soon!" he said. She waved once over her shoulder, vanishing through the terminal's electric eye, merging with other travelers.

Heidi breaks through the water, turns and breaks back again, legs churning, arms dipping up and out of sight, bare armpits, the striped white and brown of her flesh. The sound of her swimming is a comfort, at least—comfort enough, almost, to let him forget the downward spiral of his thoughts: the recollected glimpses of her he'd caught that morning as she dressed for her walk, and the skin hanging from her, wrinkled in places as if she were a wax person who'd come too near a flame. "They won't recognize you at school next week," he'd said, half to himself. "Hey, who's the toothpick lady in Associate Dean Riggs's office? Anybody know?" Then, to counter her look of weary reprobation, "Too much of a good thing, honey, is still a good thing, but it's too much." She's changed herself in the past—every few years, in fact, she's flung herself through some mini-transformation of identity or other (sculptor, Yogi, cyclist, Tarot-card reader, chicken lady), but never with such a will to self-erasure, and never with the potential for such harm to herself. They might have had children, he supposes, but for the fact she's never wanted any: *Not now, not ever.* That would have fixed her in place. But now it's too late, and her arguments against it are all so engrained in his thinking he can hardly imagine the one thing without the other, anymore: why he'd once thought he wanted a family, why she refused.

He bites off a last hunk of sandwich, feels the grains break against his teeth, the mustard with its little heat and nose-stinging tartness, his one bad tooth with the disintegrating cap giving him the intermittent ache through his jaw that he enjoys bracing himself against. Here's what she needs, he thinks: bread. Lots and lots of it. Sandwiches, croutons, rolls, croissants, pastries, French toast, buns, cinnamon twists. He checks his watch: 12:52. Swallows the last of his beer and stands to go inside for another, pausing a moment at the edge of the water and allowing his shadow to flicker over her and away again. No, let her swim, he thinks. He enjoys the crisp sound of his feet on the steps going up, and against the kitchen tiles, inside. Let her swim herself clean out of existence. See if he cares. He flips up the pop-top on his new beer with a thumb, drinks, and belches once hard. Holds a fist to his mouth though no one is here to take exception, and goes to the sunken living room window where he can watch, unseen, still drinking. Let her swim, he thinks. But the angle's wrong and he can't make out much of her from here: water sloshing up with the distant sound of her kicks now and again, or the sound of her turning. Sunlight catches in the drops of water that spray out suddenly, reminding him, as they fly, of summer days he spent as a kid (that world, where did it go?)—again the sounds of her kicking and turning. No sign of stopping.

At 1:07, his second beer gone, he returns outside. Lifts her towel from the stone table by her chair, carries it to the side of the pool and stands waiting. Birds sing. A plane buzzes by, banks and heads for the airport—one of those new stretch prop planes, part of the new millennium retro fad; he flew in one recently for a district board meeting in Seattle, and briefly now recollects the trip, the bluish morning light on board, the free drinks, and the hushed whirring of those prop blades splashing through air. One flip-turn, another, and he notes the change in her stroke, the accelerated kicks and thinner hand strokes, and knows she's ready to quit. Down she goes now— bent blurry figure hovering at the drain hole, legs scissoring open and shut, fluttering, arms sweeping wide, stretching upward; meanwhile the above-water sounds continue around him—water lapping the side of the pool, the plane more distant now—until her hands show on the ladder rail, gripping, all the bones visible.

With the water running off her and her flesh still cooled and constricting against the breeze, it should be easier not to notice, not to pay any attention. But he does notice. He can't help it. The deflated flesh just under her chin puckers, shrinks with goose flesh, and as she sucks a breath, snapping her hair side to side, her ribs loom at him. He draws a breath himself. She slouches, slumps and exhales, belly distending, and bends to dry her toes. Wraps her hair in the towel, casts him a backward glance and paces to her chair, clearing her throat once lightly in a half-curled fist. Her ass—really, he does not want to see this, has spent days trying not to see it, exactly—it's gone.

A little wrinkled skin, droopy yellowishness around her tailbone. Nothing else. So sad, so *sick,* he thinks, but forces himself to keep looking, really see.

"Home for the afternoon?" she asks. She's seated again and already reaching for the book beside her, her glasses, arranging herself on her deck chair.

"No. Just on my way right now, actually." He pauses. "Honey," he pauses again, waiting for her to look, "What are you doing?"

She raises a hand to shield her eyes from the glare. Coughs once, clears her throat. "Nothing. Reading. What are *you* doing?"

"No—I meant, what…have you looked in a mirror recently?"

She stares and says nothing. The air shifts direction between them so he no longer smells her. "All the time, honey. Every day. Every time I see you," she pulls the towel from her head and drapes it over her shoulders, "freaking *staring* at me."

Now is his chance. "Right. And for a good reason, honey. Doesn't anyone tell you? I mean, your friends, people in your book club, whatever, do they say anything? 'Cause you look…you look like…concentration camp survivors come to mind, honey. Haitian refugees…" As he speaks, she lifts her glasses to pinch the bridge of her nose and begins a tired, grating noise of disgust—a sigh escalating to a groan, louder, until finally she breaks in.

"What other people say to me or about me or behind my back is *no* special concern of mine. Give it a rest. What I wish now—what I've wished for a while now, is that you'd take a hike. Go! Find some title company bimbo to hump if you're so disappointed in…"

"Oh, so this is about…"

"No no *no*! It's not *about* anything. Whatever *it* is. Can you just…*go*…now? Please?" She visors her eyes with one hand and blinks earnestly at him. "Please?"

"No." He pauses. "In fact. Just…listen—rationally speaking I think you should…rationally speaking you might want…"

But she's glued her eyes back into her book and is moving them rapidly over the print, adamantly not hearing.

He turns and begins the march inside for his briefcase. But he can't leave it alone like that. Or, he *almost* can—that is, he can imagine another version of himself that would be able to, à la Jimmy Stewart maybe, but he isn't going to make himself that man right now, not when so much is at stake.

"You'll end up in the hospital, the way you're headed. Is that what you want?"

"If you don't kill me first with your stupid questions. Just leave me alone. I don't care, I don't care…"

"Fine. Forget I said anything. See you in the fucking morgue."

He's been bracing himself for this long in advance, really. He tells himself so as he gets in the Jeep and turns the ignition. It hasn't touched him. No, he isn't even mad. This is why he can still gear up and drive away, cool as ever, back to work, back to life. Glimpsing himself in the rearview mirror he sees his face tells a different story—his cheeks are red in splotches and his pupils have flattened to pinpricks, bending the frame of his vision out at the corners—but that's no matter; give it a few minutes, it will pass; water off a duck's back, his mother always said. "Couple of maladjusted misfits," he says. He bounces down the dirt road. Has to be hormones, mainly, making her act like this. Hell, if your body were daily eating itself out of house and home, every day stressed beyond its physical limits and deprived of carbohydrates and complex sugars to the brink of self-induced insulin shock, and forced to devour its own stored body fat in strings and globules, ribbons and chunks, cell by cell by cell digesting yourself until you were three-quarters the person you were a month ago, two-thirds the person you were a month before that, you'd snap, too. Break into an insane, liver-poisoned rant.

He glances at himself in the rearview mirror again long enough to note that his pupils are back to normal and his skin has regained its usual color. The dust tail behind him fans away, thinning in the breeze. There is again the sweet berry smell of pines mixed with burning oil and gasoline blown in through his open window.

Something Heidi said to Siam that night they were all drinking for hours on the back deck (the last happy time, he thinks now) is sticking in his head. Siam had been telling them about a man she dated all the previous fall—a former fullback for the Denver Broncos, now a consultant to a law firm specializing in sports contracts—and how, immediately following sex, and every morning as soon as he entered consciousness he'd sit straight up and say, "Hot damn! My name is…" Here he'd pronounce his name, three times, steadily building the volume, always ending with one of a handful of superlatives: *The fucking best,* or, *A-1! Rock star baby!* or, *Lick my dick!* "Crazy, huh? Imagine living with that," Siam had said, and they laughed awhile, until Heidi said, "But you know what? You know what? I *know* that feeling." Both women were on deck chairs, facing him, Heidi in a square-necked, white house dress that showed her calves nicely and the new angularity of her hips. Siam giggled some more and nodded in agreement; gave her the hang-loose sign and said, "You and me, baby." Stan swigged from his wine glass. Heidi went on, "Seriously, sometimes I wake up lately, and I think—God damn, I'm lucky. I am Heidi Riggs and this is the best I've been in years. This is my prime. Baby, I *rock.*" She wasn't looking at either of them as she said this but peering off somewhere into the darkness beyond, smiling, laughing quietly. "So, big deal—but what I want to know is, how do you *keep* that feeling. I mean, because it never lasts. On any given day it doesn't last more than a few minutes. Right? A few hours. We're so much more than just some collection of electrical impulses zinging through our bodies all the time, of course, or we'd all be Neanderthal former fullbacks. And yet…and yet, those guys are *on*to something. What do you do about the fact that all of your best feelings come out of your body, and the moment you've had them, they're gone?"

She sniffed and drifted off, savoring her next thought a moment before giving it away. "Like that morning I was out here with the mist all low on the grass and the water just flat and shiny, and there was that bald eagle there—right there," she pointed, "on the branch, staring at me—and I thought, God. That's it, isn't it. That's the answer right there, and we are all going about everything in our lives just absolutely backwards, paying attention to *all* the wrong things. We should be getting *rid* of stuff, get rid of everything, quit planning and acquiring, give up, and try to *free* ourselves until we can…" Here she lifted her shoulders slightly like she was shrugging. Her eyes fell back on them, and in a moment, having registered their estranged looks, she raised her wine glass. "Or, as my dad always says, so long as you have your health, you have everything."

"Yessiree," Stan said, and they all drank. Family, he thought— families and health and sports: it was time for the story about the day his brother ate a golf ball.

What sticks in his head now is the part about the eagle and paying attention to the wrong things—none of the sexually aggressive I-am-the-best stuff, most of which he thinks was a put-on. To renounce flesh for freedom (freedom from what, though— that was the question) you'd have to renounce the *ways* of the flesh too, right? And she isn't doing that, as far as he can tell. She's still enjoying herself plenty—lounging in the sun, reading, drinking wine straight out of the bottle, eating free-range eggs and thick cuts of bacon, steak or sausage, every morning for breakfast. She isn't giving anything up. Only carbohydrates and half of herself.

It's still stuck in his head hours later, as he makes his way home along the same roads. The sun is an hour or so from setting, but already there's a russet autumn light of earlier sunsets, and a pinch in the air that reminds him of leaves turning. Back along the county road he comes, loosening his tie at the usual milepost, yanking down to free the top button, removing the tie, undoing another two buttons, and making the turnoff to their road without downshifting, rocks and dust and dirt rooster-tailing behind him as he clatters up the hill, across the railroad tracks, thinking: *free? free from what?* Knowing, too, that freedom is always defined by its relevant confinements: only a trapped person can wish for freedom, and only a person who wishes to wish for freedom without actually having it would ever consensually trick herself into a trap in the first place—and in that case the wish for freedom is always as much a part of the confinement as anything. The trap reveals the true design of the desire, and so on. Whether or not he actually confines her is almost beside the point. If she thinks so, he does; if not, not. Most likely she doesn't want total freedom half as much as she wants to want it (or wants to *think of* herself as a person wanting it). In every case, his best plan of action will be nothing. Ride it out. Find the happy middle ground (his mother's advice to him, the day he and Heidi married: *Anytime you two have a fight, you figure out what the other person wants and where you think the middle might be...and then go about twice again as far. There's your happy middle ground—there's where you can start to talk*). If it's truly freedom she's after, nothing he can do will stop her or make her want to stay, anyway. He may as well enjoy himself, too.

THE HOUSE IS EXACTLY as he left it, dust under the empty fruit bowl on the sideboard and along the rims of the candlesticks, dishes smeared in hardened egg yolk and bacon fat on the dining room table, a jacket of hers hung over the back of one dining room chair, a sun scarf, a tube of sun block, piles of her books with papers sticking out of them on the end table next to her reading chair. *The Nothing That Is; Martin Buber; America's First Civilizations; A History of Zero; John Cage.* No sign of her. He turns on lights as he goes, room to room, picking things up. In the bathroom they share, but which is mainly hers, a knot of her hair is in the sink. He fishes it out with tissue and raises the toilet seat. The water is foul with piss, rust-colored and overlain with more tissue paper; he holds his breath a moment, tossing in the wadded hair, drops the lid back and flushes. Septic field be damned, he thinks, and holds the handle down after the toilet's empty. There's a faint floral dampness in the air so he knows she must have showered recently, within the last twenty minutes or so.

"Honey?" he says, moving into the hall outside the bathroom. "Honey? Heidi?"

The bedroom is also as he left it—bed unmade, folded laundry in piles on the dresser, dirty clothes on the floor, more of her books on the nightstand at her side of the bed. His nightstand has the clock, the phone, and an older issue of *Newsweek*. 6:22 say the enormous aquamarine numbers on the clock face. 6:23.

He finds her in the living room, on his old couch, beside the glassed shelves of elephant relics and figurines, watching a sitcom and eating turkey and ham cold cuts. She glances once at him as he comes in, and goes back to watching. Her hair is wet and she is naked. He kicks off his shoes, drops his pants, fumbles a moment hopping foot to foot to remove his boxers, and sits beside her. The sitcom is one of their favorites, a Friday night regular. She moves closer, her shoulder against his, helping him with the last buttons on his shirt, still not removing her eyes from the screen. Arms free, he tosses the shirt aside.

"What's the gag this time?" he asks.

"Oh, another re-run. The one where they can't find the man who was supposed to be working on this case for her—remember? The case of stolen identity." Heidi has another bite of ham.

He cuts his eyes at her, watches her swallow. Says he doesn't remember.

"Now she thinks she's in love with him, but she suspects him of murder, too."

"Ah, of course. Love, and lawyers, and murder—the unholy trinity of TV."

"Jesus," says Heidi. She has an astonished, rapt look on her face. "Can she get any thinner?"

"Who?" he asks. "You, or the star?"

She nudges him with an elbow. "Quit your fantasizing. She's like a twelve year-old."

"A twelve-year old with hips and big boobs, honey. Important distinction."

There's a swell of laughter from the laugh-track, and theme music to close a segment. She looks to him in an earnest, supplicating way he supposes he's meant to think of as playful; underneath it he feels how she's calculating, always calculating, for some other effect. "Think if I get some fake tits they'd pick me for her understudy? *You only get to die once...*"

"Hired!"

They laugh. She hangs a leg over his, licks the ends of her fingers and leans to put her plate on the floor. Rests her head on his chest, and again gives him the earnest, supplicating look. Nuzzles closer so the back of her head touches his chin. Her smell is thick here, though her hair is freshly washed; in another moment or two, he knows, he'll forget it or quit noticing.

"I'm sorry about today," she says.

"Sorry," he says. "What for?"

She cups his penis in her hand, presses back his foreskin and strokes him idly. "Going off like that. Telling you to leave me alone."

He waits. Parts of his body are going numb now as the pressure of her hand on him increases, his thighs, the balls of his feet, his gut, but his brain has not quit functioning. Not quite. *The trap reveals the true design of the desire*, he thinks. *And desire reveals...desire reveals the...* He can't bring the thought to any endpoint. "OK," he says. "Have you considered it, though—what I was saying?"

"Yes, I have." Her voice changes, becoming falsely cheery and upbeat. "And I've decided to go one more week. Four more pounds and one more week. After school starts, I'm back to eating like a normal person. More normal, anyway. I think I've done what I set out to accomplish, though, don't you? Down from 172 to 116 pounds? I was *fat*." She pauses, pulling once hard enough that his penis stiffens completely. She leans closer, her breath touching him.

"Your body knows best," he says.

She giggles. Slaps his leg. "*Your* body doesn't know a freaking thing sometimes, I think." She squeezes hard.

"I already told you. We had lunch once. That's all. It was very cordial, nothing special. Two martinis and a lot of suggestive remarks. On *her* part."

"I could kill you for that." Pause. "I could kill her."

"You could start by killing some of your closest friends, too, then, honey." *Or fucking them. Fuck them first, then kill them.* He doesn't say it. Almost. Checks himself just in time.

More ads flash over the screen and the scene picks up where it left off—a ritzy bar, someone singing out of tune.

She slips him into her mouth as someone on the show looses a torrent of justifications at the protagonist's client. Stan lies back, half-conscious and gazing at the assortment of elephant relics—figurines with ears, tusks, trunks in varying positions—and going back in his mind over the list of places each item came from, the better to hold off, complicate his pleasure with geography and make it last, relax the muscle groups from his back to the top of his head and let the pleasure ease slowly through him, like a golden hand: China, Burma, Samoa, South Africa, Tibet, Cambodia, Niger... Remembering, too, each one's particular history and connection with their lives—how it came to sit here, and the person or people who brought it as a gift: the college friends who'd trekked through Thai mountain country in search of a jade workshop; the Tibetan tusk carving from a woman Heidi knew slightly and which the woman had given them as thanks for some favor or other—a former student she'd helped to find a job, that was it. He remembers the woman's plucked black eyebrows and blond hair with black roots, everything about her so pert and eager to be liked. The day of each piece's arrival is imprinted somewhere there, too, in his memory. He's almost on the verge now, the cuff of pleasure tightening through his balls and thigh bones and abdomen, on into the tip of his penis—he won't last much longer. One day only: a day the sun was hard as copper on the surface of the pool and Siam had just returned from her world trek with husband number two, four figurines and a mask in a crumpled plastic bag with the print worn off, each piece wrapped in colored tissue paper, like it had been stolen or smuggled—a figurine of ivory, another of wood brocaded in beads and tiny mirrors, another of bamboo with open, arching ribs carved through to show an interior, smaller backwards-facing elephant...

"Oh no!" He remembers her hands reaching quickly to intercept broken pieces as they fell…the Rajastani clay Ganesh mask with reddish ears and tusks, crown like a miniature pagoda. Remembers standing there as she bent to lift pieces from the slate before him, gather and fit them one against the other, saying, "It's OK. Hey, look—see? We can fix it." Sunset light pulses over the mask now, glue barely visible in the fissures, the chipped bits of downward-hanging, swirling trunk and tusks where the shards were either missing or too tiny to be figured out, and pleasure leaps from him. "Yow," he says, and holds her mouth on him, fingers on her jawbones. "God damn," he says. "That was good! The best! Wow."

The picture in his head now is one from the second or third summer after they'd moved in here: Heidi during her Yoga stint, practicing breathing exercises on the edge of the diving board while he paddled around on a plastic blowup raft with his glass of hard lemonade, plunking feet and hands through the water. Though she'd begun the session by untying the strings holding in place her old daisy-patterned two-piece—unusual for her to do, at that time—he'd had to consider her essentially off-limits all afternoon, given the Yoga (possibly off the planet altogether), until once or twice, chiming in with his own *ohm's* and deep nose-breaths to mimic hers, he'd caught her eye and realized she was also partially as amused by the whole charade as he was. She'd always been. A surprise, but also not. They'd been here before—were always one way or another returning to this ironic middle ground of semi-amused playfulness and understanding which was also somehow never quite amused or understanding. He'd kicked his way over. *Namaste, naked Yogi Goddess*, he began, tracing wet fingers on her legs, scooping water over her feet and knees, *please to accept humblest compliments from Yogi admirer*. What came next merges in his memory with the hundreds (thousands?) of other times they've made love. Only the picture leading up to it, and the feeling of suddenly seeing through a charade, remain: sounds of water moving around him, sun-hot raft plastic and pool water puddling in the waistband of his trunks and under his knees, Heidi naked on the edge of the diving board, deep-breathing, legs folded together with feet crossed upward like petals.

He feels on the floor with one foot for his boxers, lifts them. "Hey, Heidi?"

She doesn't answer. Moves from him, wiping her mouth with the back of a hand.

"Hey. I know. Heidi? Let's swim." He scrubs away semen with the boxers, drops them and stands. "Let's. Come on. We haven't been in the water together all summer!"

"I just showered."

"So? It'll be fun. Come on." He lifts her from the couch—the faint dirty, fishy smell from her diet (ketonic?) clinging around her despite her just having showered, and still noticeable despite his ongoing proximity to it. He's surprised she's not lighter-feeling or easier to maneuver—surprised too that the hardness and angularity of her bones, though it's so visible, is not really evident to the touch. She feels not bony or frail, not breakable exactly, but something else…velvety and unresisting.

The sliding glass door is easy to work with the twist of one lowered wrist and he goes out, over the pebbled concrete, cool in the shadow of the carport, onto the still warm slate. At first he thinks his eyes must be fooling him—some trick of the light: the pool appears murky and gelatinous, not at all like water. Then he sees it's only the pool-cover—the bubbled plastic floating in water and sunken a few inches under in places. He lowers her at the shallow end, her feet on the steps leading in.

"Just a sec, honey," he says, and goes to reel back the cover. "Don't go anywhere." He wags a finger jokingly. The curve of her hip, how she sits, the shape of her breasts turning out to either side, it's almost how she is in the best of his memories. He watches the plastic roll aside, dividing the pool into covered and uncovered halves. There he is now, reflected in the water at his feet, familiar flesh-toned wavy smudges, submerged in the green. He doesn't look back at Heidi. He drops through the pool's reflections of himself and the evening sky, its swirled purples, pinks and blues, sun refracted through dirt and clouds. Falls as if he's dying. Sinks and hovers; hears the pump whining. Turns in the direction where he knows she is. Up again, head breaking into icy air, hands groping the rubber-treaded steps, he calls for her. "Heidi? Honey?" Water laps the side of the pool where she was sitting. He rolls onto his back, eagerly kicking his way back across and looking up through the ribbed, purple cirrus clouds. He draws a breath and sinks through darkness to the bottom. Again there's the underwater pinging of the filter. Near the drain hole and almost out of breath he turns on his back and floats, looking up. His eyes burn. Heidi is gone.

STRING

WE WERE NOT BAD KIDS. We'd never stolen candy bars, tormented insects or smaller children, drowned cats. Our worst crime the previous summer: breaking into the Cassidys' back yard to float in their pool on a moonlit night and imagine one or all of the pretty young sisters who lived there coming out to join us, or leaning from the windows of the upper story bedrooms with their hair down and the straps of their nightgowns falling away. Only their empty bathing suits on the line by the pool, smelling faintly of powder and chlorine, their shadows on the moonlit grass exciting in our imaginations too-vivid images of the bodies that would fill them later the same day, bore witness to the innocence of our transgressions. We never smoked our uncle's cigarettes or cigars, never stole his whiskey or absinthe, never drove his pickup truck through the back pasture looking for sleeping cows to tip or to detonate, though all of these things (and more) were activities considered and rejected. Once, another night not long after the swimming pool incident, we rowed his dinghy into the middle of the pond to cool off and then took turns scaring each other, standing up and causing the thing to rock wildly until, in fact, it capsized and we found ourselves suddenly waist deep in murky pond water and sinking, trying to flip the boat back over.

But aside from this, we were not bad kids. Quiet, obedient, mostly honor roll students at home. No one you'd look twice at.

Not brothers exactly, but close enough: our sister-mothers had once nearly married the same man (unbeknownst to each other) and both wound up pregnant. The rest, as they say, is history. Meanwhile, the man, our mutual father, has not been seen or heard from since the day he learned he'd managed to more or less simultaneously impregnate that pair of sisters. He must have fled the state in panicked embarrassment (possibly some terror relating to our grandfather, who was very much alive then). Sometimes we think we've spotted him at a shopping mall outside town, and once or twice on the coast. Always, our mothers are quick to say we're wrong. *No. Him? Not even close. That man? You must be kidding.* The wholesome summer months without mothers, in the heat of the upstate woods where they had spent their girlhoods, our mothers must have envisioned as some kind of corrective to their own failings as parents: a way to impose a little paternal masculinity, maybe, and rudder us back to the rustic lifestyle from which they'd so long ago defected. *Give them a bit of backbone,* they'd tell our uncle, their brother, dropping us off. *A little agrarian thrift. Teach them to hoe a row and saddle the pony. Set a trap. Survival skills! God knows they'll need them. Let them get good and dirty and cook on an open fire. Go barefoot. Square dance. Steal stuff.* That kind of thing. *Yeah, yeah, yeah,* our country uncle would say to them. *Like you ever cared about any of that before.*

To the best of our knowledge they had never, since our father's disappearance, shared another man or even dated, period. Their brother, our country uncle, was the closest thing you might say we all had to a shared male influence anymore.

But aside from the occasional, early morning fishing jaunt, Uncle Mason had no real interest in any of the activities prescribed for us by our mothers, and not much interest in us, period. Days, he spent at his insurance company in town; weekends and evenings he was in the workshop out back yowling curses and building his bad guitars and ukuleles from bubinga and exotic fruitwoods of most uncooperative grain and rarest origins. *Have you read that book about Eric Clapton's guitar?* he'd ask, if we came anywhere in sight or ear shot. *Yeah, well, you should go read it again.* Ignored and left to our own devices, we took turns swinging in the hammock, mixing pitchers of Kool-Aid and batches of Jell-O, eating pre-cooked frozen dinners and pizzas, and telling stories to scare the crap out of each other or to get each other all riled up over nothing. Girls we lusted after and fantasized about. Long dead people prying up floorboards and coming after us, clawing their way over the lawn, chasing us through the woods with clubs and bats, into the attics of abandoned old neighbor houses. Which is more or less how the myth of the flaming ghost-in-the-road ever got started. There was no local mythology attached to her, no ancient folklore-type narrative. One of us saw her in a dream and remembered hearing of her from some older kids at school who'd played the same prank, but differently. *By the time you see her it's too late, rising in the light of your high beams like a headless flaming little witch, arms beckoning you on…no, like a little bloody white rabbit someone's strung up on a line and lit on fire. You see her and you know it's too late. Bat-a-bing, bat-a-bubinga. You're a dead man.* And on rainy days, backgammon in the musty library. Books and more books and endless games of solitaire when the heat was too much; and when we could no longer bear another minute's silence in each other's company, the grandfather clock sawing out the boards of eternity, tick by monotonous tick in the background, when some form of physical release was positively required, lame tennis matches on Mason's weed-festooned clay court, whacking at each other tennis balls so dead and bald they looked more like mushrooms than any kind of sporting goods. Hit hard enough, one would occasionally pop wide, emitting an eggy smell of rubberized glue, ancient pine needles, and chilly spring rain.

You could say it was her fault, Ms. Flaming-Ghost-in-the-Road: certainly that was how we thought of it. Because once we decided it was our job to make her real again, everything was out of our hands. Like she was telling us how it should be done and giving us all necessary instructions—the angle of the sunset and time of day, which telephone pole to string her from and how to bunch her at the top like a thing with a severed head. Where to smear her with currant jelly and motor oil. You could say we had no part in it, really, once the plan was in motion; and then at the sound of the car approaching—the one, the fated moment bearing down—both of us knowing, simultaneously, it would work. I was on signal duty, closer to the road and watching, arm up, ready to wave *when*, Pete ten paces back in the woods, string in hand. Headlights reflected on the leaves overhead. Light in the asphalt. Motor coming closer, a chirp in the engine noise audible now, a radio playing, tires on gravel, fan belt clacking, and then the moment: down went my arm, Pete yanked her line, and up she flew, alive, floating into the headlights so real and bloody I thought I heard her scream and then…

…tail lights stabbing half-darkness, groaning sound of tires on gravel and gravel sliding away, shattering glass and underbrush, the groaning noise of metal scraped into and colliding against something final—tree stump, boulder—both of us again looking at each other and knowing: we had done something finally, really, terribly wrong. Terribly and irrevocably wrong. And then we were running.

SHE THOUGHT OF CALLING him from the truck stop greasy spoon with the latest progress update. "Guess where I am?" she might begin. "A few more hours…a little starchy deep-fried goodness here, and back on the road." The pay phone at her table seemed placed there purposely to remind her, beckon, to cause this temptation, though she knew, of course, it was not. It was for the convenience of lonely long-haul truckers trying to make the most of a single rest stop— shower, crap, eat, rest, phone home. But the whorled handprints, smeared and hardened in jelly, pancake syrup, or motor oil, gave it such an aura of easy, friendly usedness. Why not call? Say a few cheerful, excited things to him like any ordinary traveler on her way to an ordinary loved one, kicked back like a trucker with her feet up on the opposing seat, chatting away. No. It had been her plan to keep the arrival time unknown, leave her cell phone off and stowed deep in her purse. Surprise him, catch him off guard. Like in the beginning. Anyway, there was nothing ordinary about this journey, or its purpose. She'd do well to remember that and to remember, more generally, that there was so much more to her than what she was beginning to conclude were the *very* limited ways in which he allowed himself to consider her anymore, the result of their having dated and more or less cohabited the last eight months, and of his having become, finally, accustomed enough to her idiosyncrasies, likes and dislikes, work schedule, her whole general *presence*, that she was finally (she suspected) nothing to him but a huge and invisible bore. A dull but once somewhat-beloved distraction and obligation, with a vagina. No, dammit! There was so much more to her than that—a whole past and future! A lifetime of friends and incidents and feelings, dating, music, recipes, school, trips, cars owned, jobs, days passed, hopes and plans and dreams. Only…he didn't really *care* about any of that. It made his eyes glaze and roll up in his head hearing it. "These details," he'd tell her. "Yes, where you learn to cook and your first head chef's job, yes, how you make your way in the man's world, they are fascinating one by one. Together they are so many ways the same thing over and over and over again. For me, anyway, it is the same." Her friends had warned her: *Just don't let him paint you, Ginny. Once you've done that, it's over.* Was that it? Her vanity and folly, insisting that he live with her, paint her, adore her, memorize her life story *and* still find her fascinating enough to be mated together for…forever? For life? Was she really that hopeful? The painting itself—this, another thought to tuck away fast; she really did not want to remember—had born so little likeness to her she could barely look. Her arms and legs maybe, emblazoned in sloppy, sludgy colors and too-evident brush strokes; cryptic, vase-shaped, flowering thing at the center of it all, leaking blood and festooned as an alien from space. A thing with horns and tentacles. *That* was her? How he saw her? She had asked him to show her *this*, this way of seeing that was in itself an aberration and a violation of anything good and decent in the world?

So she resisted: the phone with its friendly, familiar stamp of handprints and finger whorls, well grimed keypad and too-often coiled and uncoiled heavy duty cord. Held it once to her ear and imagined the sound of his voice: his lulling Russianisms, buzzing nasality, the humor nestled there mysteriously, charmingly, in the soft bones of the palate alongside all his half-intended mispronunciations and mis-implications. And then (because she had a good and accurate enough imagination to know exactly how it would play out) the tired exhale when he heard she was actually on her way to him now, hours away…too soon, too early in the summer, before the most recently agreed upon visitation date, before he'd finished anything close to enough "work." The tired intake of breath letting her know there was really no room in the cabin; busy or not, telecommuting to work or not, she'd be underfoot. "Yes, we already talk about this, though," he'd say, pausing long enough to allow her to read whatever she liked into it, "I miss you as well. I am here lonely as a bear. But…" Here she could even picture how he'd draw up his shoulders and gesticulate faintly. "It is better this way, I think, for now." The excellent meals she'd envisioned them sharing, nothing but a nuisance, a grid forced upon his days, a clock to keep, plank to walk…

But no. She was not *just* on her way now to cozy up with him for fun summer times. She was, in fact, on a fact-finding mission for her own clarification, her own edification, whether or not he approved. She had to remember: she was on her way now bringing news, to see what was what, and, in all likelihood, to get back in the Audi and drive home again, south and west; to figure out what came next all on her own. It was over, really. It had been over since the day he left (earlier, probably: the day he finished his so-called painting, or maybe earlier even than that)—his last words, squinting at her apologetically through the open window of his car as he got ready to throw it in reverse and back out of her driveway a final time: "Yes, sure. When you want, when you can, you come north. Because it is terribly bo-o-o-oring for you, I think. Nothing to do but listen to frogs at night and read books all day. So many bugs! But of course I love it, so… Only if you want to come, yes. If you want. When you can, then it is good. You are busy girl too. Otherwise, we see each other again one day when I am back, okey-doke?"

It shouldn't have surprised her. No one who knew her was surprised.

Before their cohabitation, he'd lived alone in the one-bedroom walkup of a mutual friend of theirs who'd suddenly and without cause flown town. Marcy. Gone back west, where she came from. Phone, power, heat, water, garbage, all had been in Marcy's name, and were transferred to him. The deal, he told her, the afternoon she came around looking for Marcy and found instead this craggy, T-shirted man with his unshaven cheeks and beguilingly sad eyes, cigarette breath, arms deliciously roped in blue veins, the deal was he could stay here as long as he wanted—stay out the lease, anyway, which would expire the end of that month—so long as he took over all utilities and upkeep. But he did not prefer to. Did not see the point in, "How you say…needless expense for the overheads. Better this way, and more cheap. So I call phone company, I call gas and electric. No more," he said, showing her to what had been Marcy's bedroom. The floors were now draped in paint-spattered old sheets, painted and prepped canvases of various sizes leaning, back-side-out, in every corner, easels, paint brushes end-up in coffee cans, tubes of paint everywhere, books piled in little towers on the floor. No furniture but a single bare mattress. None of Marcy's old shag throw rugs, floor pillows and too-cushiony fold out Ikea chairs and couches, her endless scented pillar candles. He pointed: from the window ledge to the street below ran a line of white string, attached, at the window casement, to the handle of a cracked and paint-splotched hand bell hung on a hook. "My connection to outside world. Cracked like Liberty Bell, yes?" he said, and illustrated for her, causing the bell to clang spastically. "If one of my friends wants me, old friends visiting from out of town, say, with some vodka or something good to drink, we go together… Any time at all, day or night…here," again he caused the bell to clang, and this time grinned provocatively, showing for the first time his many ruined, missing and stained teeth. "Because I *love* people and I am always here alone, so…I hear bell, I run like school boy. You come by once, I show you. We have some wine and look…" Here he gestured toward his canvases. "Yes?"

"But what a way to live!"

"Yes. It is not so much. But is mostly OK, I think."

"What's wrong with a cell phone?"

"I have one of these too," he said, and whisked an older Nokia from inside his paint spotted jeans pocket. "I love it so much." He kissed the phone and flipped it open. "But the battery. You see. Yes, battery is dead. Again, no power. And I think, maybe it didn't work anyway. One day though. Yes? It can work."

She'd never considered herself an easy catch, but this once… Well, he'd seemed so lost and harmless. Vulnerable. And with those horrible teeth. The care he took later—when she, in fact, came to visit and the wine led to the paintings which led to more talk which led, naturally, to the lone grubby mattress on the floor—finger raised for a moment to still her and then bouncing naked across the floor to unhook the loop end of the string from the bell handle and to anchor it to another hook, but bell-less, beside the bell. "Busy signal, yes?" he said, again animating his face to show his pleasure and bouncing back to where she lay under the grimy sheet. And still later, lying beside him in the absolute dark, no light switch anywhere to relieve it, no sound of air conditioning, heating, refrigerator, fan, ventilation. Nothing. Dead still and calm. Only the street noise from below and then the sound that had wakened her—a faint buzz-buzz-thrum. The string still unhooked from the bell, she saw it then in the moonlight or the streetlight or some combination of the two, quivering with tension and then slackening, that tension singing its fierce faint buzz-buzz-thrum sound, harder, and harder again. Someone wanted him. Two a.m. and someone was down there pulling that string for all it was worth. And then nothing at all. String slack again. Yes, she'd thought. She could get to like this artsy bohemian way of life— camping out in the dark with candles and take-out food. No way for anyone in the world to reach her, unless she chose to be reached. No way for anyone to find her or suspect her presence. *How romantic…* she could imagine Marcy saying. Not tomorrow, but soon, she'd have to call her, fill her in: say, *That man in your apartment…what used to be your apartment, that is? Well!* Why had it all changed so much—all the easy, natural, out-of-each-other's way sexiness, night after night, whenever she felt like it, cooking for him on her campout stove and throwing away whatever they didn't finish—and when? Where did all that *fun* go? Why, as soon as the lease was up and he'd moved his paintings across town to her apartment, why the feelings of doom and entrapment lying beside him in her own bed under clean sheets and puffy comforters, the heated air moving in currents around them, the good clean smells of her own home, its working utilities and flushable toilets, why had all of it felt so…claustrophobic? She'd known, even then, watching him beside her on his back in her bed and staring up into the dark, freshly showered, that he'd never stay, except to convenience himself; he'd never be kept. Only for now, because he liked her at least that much and had nowhere else to go, nowhere to be until summer again and his cabin on the lake in the Adirondacks. "Shack really, though I like it better this word, *cabin,* yes? More romantic." It had been such a long way in the future. Or had seemed so at the time.

And now here was the future, the last few hours of it before she was with him again, the road ahead red with sunset light, almost impossible to see through the glare. Light exposing every fissure and ding in her windshield, every blasted-apart bug, and the smeared tracks her wipers had worn in the glass. Poor enough visibility that she almost missed the turn off and then the rural route up over the hill to the next interstate, thinking, *A life! New life inside me and new life stretching out ahead, with or without Dmitri.* And that was the tricky part. That one word: *without.*

THE TRUCK WOULD BE ALL RIGHT. Some fresh dents to the front bumper, new scratches, busted side window and shattered headlight. Nothing beyond repair. He'd cranked the engine on and off twice to be sure, gotten out and circled around as far as he could, assessing things: the stand of birches overhanging the ravine against which the truck's front left bumper seemed now more or less permanently wedged; the sound of the creek, invisible below; the two tires, one front, one back, still on solid ground. It'd be fine. Might cost him, getting it out. Then again, there was the balance due to him still from Weiders for that roofing job on their garage last spring. *Catch up with me later, man*, he'd told them. *Hard times for everyone…and my truck's about to drop a tranny any day. Could work it as a trade.* True, he'd been not quite a month longer than expected finishing the job, and some of the flashing had not turned out picture perfect, he'd give them that, but it was tight. Didn't leak. They owed him. Now would be time to call in that favor. Have Weider park his service truck up on the road, tie off to his rear bumper, block his own wheels and winch him up gingerly from above. And when all four wheels were back on terra firma, get in and rev her back up the slope.

"Stupid, stupid, *stupid*," he said, walking now, head throbbing, and wishing (again) he could just have back those crucial few seconds when the thing, whatever it was, bounced up from the pavement in the middle of the road causing him to wince and jerk his head to the side, yank at the steering wheel and stomp his feet on the brake and clutch. All the wrong instincts, wrong reflexes, wrong timing. Should have driven right through it instead. Run the damn kids over, if he could find them.

Blood trickled in one eye and he flicked it aside, pressing lightly where the ache felt most centralized, just above his hair line, where he must have smacked into the steering wheel. Dull, sticky, aching flesh. First things first, then: get to the emergency room. Have them stitch him up and send him on his way with new pain killers. Good ones like hydros or vicodin. Later would come the air-conditioned chill of his doublewide and the sagging loveseat there by the TV.

The rack of cold Molsons in his fridge and the queasy, enervated drift, beer after beer mixed with the painkillers; getting up from the loveseat, going on numb feet up the three steps to the kitchenette and back down, hurling his weight into the loveseat—bandaged and stitched and calm—injury providing the all-bases-covered excuse for this bender and for days of missed work and for the other thing he guessed would eventually follow, probably with beer number four or five: the call to Karen at her parents'. She'd need to know about it, after all, so as not to alarm her later, the ER service likely showing up on her insurance statement. They might even require notification before admitting him. *Paid the fifty bucks deductible co-pay thing myself so no worries there, babe, shouldn't show as nothing more than services rendered. Nah, I'm fine now*, he'd say. *Had a little wreck. Pranked by some kids, if you can believe—you know, that old one with some rags and fishing line? Carl Dobson's boys is my bet. Ha ha ha. Split my head wide open like a melon. Like that what's-his-name that one time in high school, remember...? Fourteen stitches and bled out about a gallon. Vicodin or some shit, I forget, I wasn't paying attention... Thing is, I miss you so much it don't even matter, don't touch it. Nothing does...* No, stop right there; anything but that. Because all he'd get in response would be the same as before and the same as ever: *I miss you too, James. Course I do. Miss our whole lives together. How could I not? You're like a part of me. But there's no way of turning back the clock and nothing to do about that and all our bad history anymore. You gotta see. There's no other way for me. So we treat each other kind—move on. I'm sorry, but babe, you gotta stop calling. It don't change anything...* The way the narcotics would wind together with the beer, the bitter aftertaste of pills in each breath and that stinging sourness in the back of his throat, the lush weight through his blood, sweet chemicalized dizziness, and then sleep. That was all he craved now. Positively craved and deserved, really. Forget Karen.

He crashed through the last bit of undergrowth and out to the road, staggering once against the hardtop. Open, cooler air, stiller somehow, and overhead the sky visible in a stripe where the trees had been cut back—dusky gloaming blue of early night. Power lines humming. Yellow paint down the middle of the road. Macadam emitting tar smells and reflecting warmth up to his knees. Huge and wobbling, the shadow of himself that loomed across the road, arms outstretched, and before he could block it here came the childhood memory he was always trying to stuff down and forget, but from which he was never exactly free: his uncle's shadow in the living room window that day swinging giddily where shadows didn't belong, making him laugh as he ran up the steps and inside, anticipating some hilarious new joke. *Uncle Edgar, look at Uncle Edgar! Crazy, crazy Eggy!* Only it was no joke, no spinning plates or juggled pillows, singing wineglasses, one-armed chin ups, disappearing coins or cards, sticks balanced on the end of his nose. Just Edgar's shoes at chin height, improbably tied and polished, puffy white tube socks pulled high and showing below the cuffs of his pants; face black and swollen, slacks tented around his crotch. Seeing that, the erect penis, he'd again almost been certain it was a joke—an elaborate, black-hearted joke, but still a joke—except for the face, the color of the skin, and the rope cutting so uncompromisingly into the neck. It was not a joke. And after a while, after he'd waited long enough in silence to be absolutely sure, he'd stolen back out and down the front steps in search of an adult. It was this same hour of day— early evening passing into night, no stars yet but a blue-black sky of luminous orange and gold clouds, his own shadow hunched and moving ahead of him on the ground, stretching longer and doubling itself and then foreshortening again with each buzzing streetlight he passed. Everything he encountered had seemed somehow altered in his perceptions—heightened, clarified by these exciting (because unexpected) new feelings of power and purposefulness. He'd seen Uncle Edgar hanging from the high beam in his own living room. He was on his way now to tell them all, the adults, about it—bearer of the news.

To mark the place, because he couldn't be sure of skid marks in this light, or of a visible enough break in the undergrowth at the side of the road by which to relocate the truck later, he removed his shirt and wove it through the branches of a low growing sumac bush. Lifted the bottom of his undershirt and pressed hard where the pain pulsed most intensely and was sure, releasing it, that he'd only made things worse, torn away some protective clotting or abraded the numbing, traumatized tissues. So there was now a layer of eye-stinging sensation atop the aching throb. *Quit*, he told himself. *Leave it alone. Don't touch, don't panic. Just wait. Someone will be along. It's a busy enough road. Someone will pick you up, get you to the hospital. Sure. Have to be somebody I know, looking like…like a zombie. Who'd stop for a zombie?* He held his arms out and shuffled jerkingly up the road a few steps like a mis-strung marionette. "OOOhhhh," he moaned. "I will eat your brains, you pussy Dobson boys. I will kill you and suck up your brains like warm milkshakes. I'm coming for you now. You'd better run. Run for your lives."

THE MAN COVERED in his own blood had not given a name or any of the details of his situation; yet here he was beside her, in the soft dashboard light as she sped down the mountain, moaning quietly now and then and holding to his forehead what, in other circumstances, would have served a most intimate purpose. The absurdity of it! Because now of all times when she no longer needed an emergency stash of pads and Tampons, one had proven essential. And to aid a perfect stranger. Between corners she stole glances to be sure he was all right still, and conscious.

"Hang in there," she said. "You're sure you're OK?"

He nodded. "Got a boner."

"Excuse me?"

"I said. I'm not a goner."

"Anything at all I can do for you?"

"I appreciate your stopping for me. Them Advils haven't touched it, but I ain't surprised. You wanna turn here on 47. We're almost there."

He'd shown up in her headlights just past what she assumed was the top of the mountain, following a brief straightaway and an incongruous stretch of white-washed, New England-style picket fence at the side of the road. His face, at first sight, off-puttingly familiar or recognizable—someone she'd known from long ago or known all her life—until she came closer and could fully identify what she was seeing: blood. A bleeding man in a T-shirt and jeans, looking as if he'd just had a bucket of carnage poured on him. He was familiar because he was the stock image of suffering from religious paintings, horror movies, news clips—image of the savior crucified, blood streaming down his cheeks and temples; sole survivor of a crash. She'd seen him a million times in different contexts but never *him* specifically, whoever he was. Slowing, stopping, lowering the passenger side window, she leaned to address him: "Oh my god. Everything all right?" Stupid question. "I mean, what…happened? Let me help."

"Wrecked," he said. "Ain't as bad as it looks, I'm sure, but I need to get to the hospital in Marion. Can you…?"

"Of course. You just tell me where, I'm not from here. Get in."

And then he was in the car beside her, panting almost, hands gripping his thighs, skinny thighs she noted, deflated looking really, spindly as spoon stems, and there was a boil at the end of his nose. No, not a boil, something else—an abrasion or a clump of body matter, congealed blood, stuck to him. She searched her purse for anything in the way of First Aid supplies, anything to help clean up—creams, bandages, painkillers.

"Nice…car," he'd said. "Probably gonna wreck it."

"Not to worry. Here," she said. "Advil." Shook out four tablets for him. "Can you dry swallow? And this… I'm afraid it's the best I have, sorry, but it should—" she laughed once "—at least it'll be fairly absorbent." She unfolded the pad, the familiar floral soap and baby powder antiseptic smell of it reminding her, as always (and incongruously), of Tom Robbins, cowgirls, being a teenager, wishing she were a cowgirl with enormous thumbs hitching her way to freedom and adventure. She leaned from her seat. "Here," she said. "Closer. No, wait. Let me see." She hit the overhead passenger's side light. "Lower your head just slightly and I'll... Oh, I...can see it now." She hoped her voice didn't give away too much concern: the sight of the blood coursing there in the blood-thickened hair and the grayish aspect of what she was pretty sure, underneath, must be his skull, sticking through, visible momentarily as she moved aside hair to see where exactly the worst of it might be. "Apply pressure, but not too hard. There." And she placed it firmly against his head. Stopped at his sudden hissing intake of breath. "OK?"

"Yeah. Hurts is all."

"You'll be all right. Just keep up that pressure. Not too much. And maybe..." She'd been about to tell him the only other thing she remembered from her advanced life saving classes in high school, *elevate the wound site*, when she realized there was not much point saying *that*; his head was by default elevated, unless he fainted or fell over in which case she had no idea what to do next, anyway. "They bleed a lot," she said. Another piece of First Aid information resurfacing unexpectedly. "Head wounds. Even superficial ones. Because of the number of veins and capillaries so close to the surface of the skin? Not a lot of skin there to keep things together anyway. A little cut loses a lot of blood. But you'll be fine. I'm sure."

"Are you a doctor?"

"God no! I cook. I run a restaurant...some restaurants."

"Drive a *doctor's* car." Something in his tone was abruptly discouraging, enough so almost to make her reconsider her spirit of volunteerism. Not that she felt threatened (what could he do, after all?), but there was a mocking quality all too transparently connected with enviousness or spite and self-pity, which she'd encountered often enough to identify, though still it surprised her and she'd never learned any good ways of deflecting it. *You drive a nice car*, was really only a step or two away from, *You drive a nice car, you must think you're better than me*, and was really only a nudge further from *Give me your car, I deserve it too*. No, that wasn't it either: she was discouraged because she was reminded of Dmitri again. Dmitri who had insisted, whenever they went together anywhere, that they ride public transit or take his old beater Plymouth. Never the Audi. If she looked back on their time together she could think of maybe one or two evenings which had involved transport in the Audi. And those had seemed to her start-to-finish permeated by such cartoonishly miserable looks from him she couldn't help imagining the caption you'd write beneath the image they made together: *Sullen Russian expat meets spoiled American girl*. Might as well stay home. But this, obviously, was an old problem encroaching upon a new situation and unrelated to the bleeding man.

"Seat belt," she'd said, and sat back, belted in herself, ready to go. Watched him struggle momentarily, one-armed, to pull the belt around and hook it, then, switching hands, still holding the pad to his head, struggling to get the thing attached. "Hell," she said and again leaned from her seat, close enough to feel surrounded by him, the heat and smell of his blood, the sight of the wound pushing up in her memory as she pressed the seat belt catch and tried to make it engage. "Screw it," she said, and released. Put the car in gear, lifted her foot from the brake and rolled ahead. "Not like we're likely to crash a second time tonight, right? Between the two of us we must have used up our nightly quota of bad driving luck. Wouldn't you say?"

He grunted.

"Maybe our nightly quota of bad luck, period?" But saying that was inviting more, anticipating it. Because truthfully she knew what was ahead with Dmitri and knew it was not good luck of any kind. It was no kind of luck, actually; it was running straight into a brick wall. Because he'd tried to leave, had really slithered off in his own vaguely harmless, passive way, never making any promises, and all she was going to prove, chasing him down to tell him she was pregnant, was... Well, that was the part she didn't know yet. But she was quite sure it wouldn't end happily.

"If you say."

"So where am I going?"

"Straight on like you were," he said. "We'll hit Marion in about ten-fifteen minutes and I'll tell you where to next. If you see anything jump up in front of your headlights, like a ghost or something, just keep going. Don't stop."

"Excuse me?"

And then he'd told her how it had happened: the Dobson boys—*six or eight of them, who the hell remembers*—and Carl Dobson, his own former high school rival—*fell in love with the same girl; I'll let you guess who got her*—now somehow connected with the local Lutheran bible camp and never home all summer, so the boys were always at loose ends and getting up to no good. "Blew a cow apart one time."

"Did what?"

"Sure. You stick some M-80's up its ass and light 'em. Blam. Instant Sloppy Joe."

"That's disgusting!"

"Sorry. I forgot you're a cook."

"Good grief. You think that's only disgusting because I'm a *cook?*"

"I guess I don't know what's disgusting to anyone else to hear. I'm just saying. It's kind of a disgusting turn of phrase."

"Well fine. So what was it they did this time?"

And he told her about the ghostly thing flying up in his windshield like it had dropped from the sky, a little white witch, white cephalopod covered in blood, something totally weird, and too late, realizing it was only a prank—one he'd heard of, as a kid, and considered pulling himself. "But I kinda lost my taste for pranks after a certain age, I guess. Lost my ability to see the humor in that type of behavior, really. Anyhoo. I hit the brakes and cornered a little too hard you know, and kind of slid out of control. Couldn't bring her back around. That's it. Straight off the road. Somewhere along the way," he pointed at his head, "the collateral damage."

She nodded.

And now here they were on highway 47, almost to Marion. Still she didn't have a name for him. "Holding up OK?" she asked again.

He grunted and she reached for him without looking or thinking. Found his hand, turned it over in hers and squeezed, moved from there up his forearm and again squeezed. Glanced at him and realized with some alarm that what she had thought was a boil or clump of matter on his nose was actually his nose itself, a bone or some piece of it broken off and sticking through flesh. Felt her hamburger and greasy fries, ranch-drenched iceberg lettuce, surge slightly higher against her esophagus where they'd been lurking all this time, barely contained at the base of her throat. "I'll let you in on a little…" she began, and stopped herself. Habit. Because of Dmitri always telling her, *Don't. Why talk so much? Sometimes less you say is actually more. But Ginny, she gets in a situation where she is…how you say…a little more worry than normal, and she want to talk. Just talk and talk. Like everyone want to hear how you walk to work last week and what you say to so-and-so and how many plates you serve last weekend. I think is special kind of American solipsism really…* And then it was perfectly clear to her (though for a moment only) how it would be a relief cutting off from him—boor with his caramel rot-stained teeth and refusal to wear antiperspirant or use toothpaste. Who needed his particular opinions about anything? *Staggeringly bad taste in men*, her mother had always said to her. *The worst of the worst, every time. I mean if there was a man with bubonic plague you'd find him and bring him home for his charming sores. Why, Ginny? Where did we go wrong?* "So," she began again, "I'll let you in on a little secret. Where I was…"

The bleeding man snorted suddenly and held a hand to his mouth. "Holy Christ, there's a lot of blood here all of a sudden… what the…"

"Where?"

"Like *everywhere*! I don't know…down my throat. Shit. It's so sudden." He paused, sputtering, swallowing. "I'm drowning!"

"No, you aren't! Don't say another thing."

He pointed wildly at the blue H sign as they entered town.

"I see!" Again, without looking or thinking she grabbed at his arm, his shoulder, squeezing. Kept her hand there. Rubbed instinctually, patted him and rubbed some more, felt his blood warm and sticky between her fingers. "OK, it's going to be OK. You'll see. It'll be all right." The muscles were so like Dmitri's but not, same shape and size more or less, but not as yielding. Rigid. Like bricks. Like a man going into shock? "Hang in there! Can you do that for me? Hold on!"

RUNNING AND RUNNING. Jumping old stone walls and falling through moldy-smelling patches of ancient blow-down, caught for moments at a time and plunging on, uphill, whipped in the face by low hanging branches. Up and up, to the bald point of the hill where quartz and granite boulders loomed like half-buried animals, whales and giant sea turtles, and from here veering southward to more familiar ground again: the tractor trail and then the dirt road which eventually connected to the lane bisecting Uncle Mason's property. Slowing now because it was clearer to us no one had followed: we would not be caught. The hollowed thump of blood in our heads and mad chirp of wind in our ears, throats too ragged from breathing to talk yet…all of it the remnants of an expired call to alarm. We stopped. Held still. No other sound. No feet cracking branches behind us, no voices. Only the hoo-hoo-ooo of an owl and other beginnings of night noises in the woods. Trees around us faded to silver and seemed more distant in the vanishing light. So we were OK after all, alone and no longer even in danger of getting lost. We'd been out this far at night before and never failed to get home.

And now walking again, stumbling down the dirt road and almost in sight of Mason's back pasture, his woodworking shop there at the end of his lane, the new worries set in: because we were not bad kids. We'd done bad things, yes, but never anything as seemingly out of control or destructive as what had happened tonight. We could not believe ourselves capable of causing another person harm.

Not deliberately. Yet the question remained: what if? What if there was no sound of footsteps following, no thump-thump of someone giving chase, no voices yelling after us *stop, come back or suffer the consequences*, what if all of this was because the driver of the vehicle we'd pranked was now dead? Worse: injured and slowly dying?

We had to find out.

"First though, a little liquid courage." This was Pete.

"Absolutely."

Where to find it, we knew. Knew where the skeleton key dangled from a green shoestring nailed in the hollow of the mostly dead apple tree across from Mason's workshop; knew that at the back of his workshop were the gallon jugs of straight grain alcohol. *Because I have a license for it. For varnishes and French polishing and to bend wood in the heat of an alcohol lamp if I need to, and for whatever else I want it for. But you listen closely, because I mean every word I'm about to say: I measure it. Every drop. And I do mean every drop. It's a legal liability, and anyway, the stuff isn't cheap. So either of you touches any, I'll have your skin or at the very least send you packing. Got it?*

In we went, careful to close the door but not lock it behind us. Of course, we wouldn't throw on any of the crazy flood lights in the front room of his workshop. That'd be giving ourselves away instantly. Through the dark we went, deftly winding between his backs and sides and clamps and jigs, his giant saws and routers and other machines we didn't know the names for. *Here is one man's fortune*, he'd told us, an afternoon early on. *One man's complete and total net worth that is, aside from the house. Net worth...or maybe folly. Can you put a price on a man's dreams? Sure. I guess. In this case, about a hundred-sixty, -seventy grand. I have no living dependents and no one on whom to spend a penny, so this is it, where it goes. This hobby, this... whatever you want to call it. Art form? Habit. I didn't say I was any good either, and I've never expected a dime in return. I just wanted to have a shot at making some decent guitars, and I wanted the best and latest to do so. You know, my job in town. I make a little money. Every year, a little more. So.... Wood like this, do you have any idea what it goes for? A book-matched old growth set like this?* So on.

Presuming ourselves safe in the windowless back room, we pulled on the string of the old bare-bulb overhead light and watched its shadow twirl on the floorboards. But the bottles were not here— thick, gallon jugs with ring handles you could hardly fit two fingers through—he'd moved them or we'd misremembered. Or he'd found some new better set of techniques which didn't involve distilled spirits of the highest possible grade. And then it was too late anyway because we heard his footsteps on the stairs coming up. His key in the rattly old door and then the door flying open. Bang. Mason in a rage because he knew his shop like he knew the shape of his own chin in a mirror and must have understood immediately, from the way that door opened and from the light in the back room (obviously, he would not have left it on), that its sanctity had been violated. Lights sprang up everywhere, impossibly bright, flooding every fiber, stain and grain of visible reality with illumination, because this was his prerogative: light by which to polish a piece of spruce or bubinga or koa wood until he could read the brand name of the specialty light bulb company itself reflected in the gloss. *"You boys, get out here now before I find you and tan the hide off you. Both. Now."* We didn't know then, though it might not have comforted us much, knowing, that six months from now a woman we'd never met, and who we would not meet until early the following summer applying for jobs at her newly opened roadside café—a complete stranger, the course of whose life we'd inadvertently redirected that night using a rag and a piece of string—would lie under lights at least this bright or brighter, legs open in the birthing position, and yowling louder than either of us had ever heard a person yowl; that the forceps used in clamping the umbilical cord of her first born would be the same set of forceps (it was a small country hospital, after all) used months prior first to set the stitches and then pull them from the head of the man who loomed over her, coaching her through these last moments of delivery, and whose life they both had to believe she had saved on a country road (and only because she'd stopped for fries and a burger, and stayed a little longer than necessary thinking about calling the man she then loved, the man whose child had just uttered its first fierce and despairing cry of … joy?). All of this, a set of possibilities unknown to us, and a future set in motion by our own selfish, half-considered actions. No help to us whatsoever as we collapsed against each other in sweaty anticipation of what was next. *"I mean it. Out here now or you're both dead. On the count of three. One. Two..."*

ACKNOWLEDGMENTS

I'd like to thank the Washington State Artist Trust and Eastern Washington University Office of Grants and Research for support while working on many of these stories.

For line edits, editorial insights, and advice, special thanks to editors Carolyn Kuebler, Stephen Donadio, and Linda Swanson-Davies. For all of that, and for assembling the book into some semblance of order, huge thanks to Victoria Barrett.

As always, boundless loving thanks to Ann Joslin Williams, lifelong reading/writing friend, whose willingness to critique draft after draft of these stories informs every story.

And to my wife, Caridwen Irvine-Spatz, for her patience, faith, inspiration, and advice on all matters, story-related and not story-related…and for the opening lines to at least a few of the stories here.

ABOUT THE AUTHOR

Born in New York City, Gregory Spatz holds degrees from Haverford College, University of New Hampshire, and The University of Iowa Writers' Workshop. He now lives in Spokane, Washington, where he teaches in the MFA program at the Inland Northwest Center for Writers, Eastern Washington University. Spatz spent his youth in New England, mostly in the Berkshires.

He is the author of the novels *Inukshuk*, *Fiddler's Dream*, and *No One But Us*, as well as a short story collection, *Wonderful Tricks*. His short stories have appeared in *The New Yorker*, *Glimmer Train Stories*, and *New England Review*, among others, and he has published numerous book and music reviews for *The Oxford American*. He is the winner of a 2012 NEA Literature Fellowship.